BANISHED FROM THE HERO'S PARTY,
I Decided to Live a Quiet Life in the Countryside

5

ZAPPON

Illustration by
Yasumo

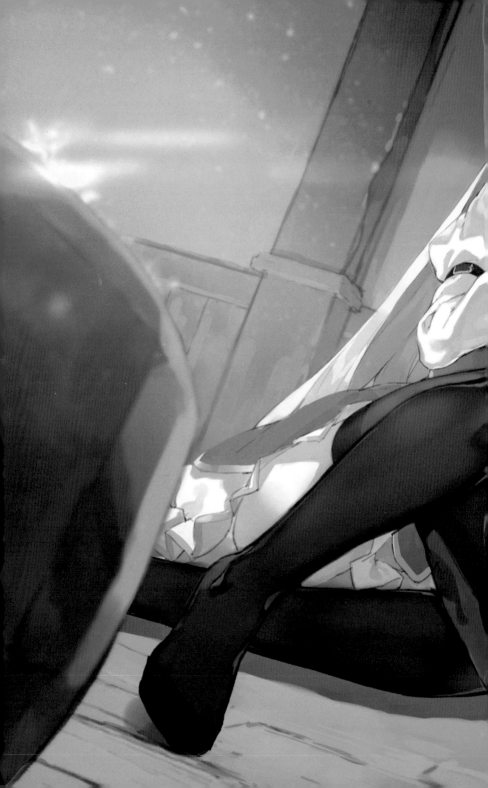

"You're blushing, Red."

CONTENTS

Illustration: Yasumo
Design Work: Shindousha

"If we had met under different circumstances, do you think we might have ended up together?"

BANISHED FROM THE HERO'S PARTY,

I Decided to Live a Quiet Life in the Countryside

5

ZAPPON

Illustration by
Yasumo

YEN ON

New York

Banished from the Hero's Party, I Decided to Live a Quiet Life in the Countryside, Vol. 5
Zappon

Translation by Dale DeLucia
Cover art by Yasumo

▼ ▼

SHIN NO NAKAMA JYANAI TO YUUSHA NO PARTY WO OIDASARETANODE, HENKYOU DE SLOW—LIFE SURUKOTO NI SHIMASHITA Vol. 5
©Zappon, Yasumo 2019
First published in Japan in 2019 by KADOKAWA CORPORATION, Tokyo.
English translation rights arranged with KADOKAWA CORPORATION, Tokyo through TUTTLE-MORI AGENCY, INC., Tokyo.

Yen On
150 West 30th Street, 19th Floor
New York, NY 10001

Visit us at yenpress.com
facebook.com/yenpress
twitter.com/yenpress
yenpress.tumblr.com
instagram.com/yenpress

First Yen On Edition: February 2022

Yen On is an imprint of Yen Press, LLC.
The Yen On name and logo are trademarks of Yen Press, LLC.

▼ ▼

Library of Congress Cataloging-in-Publication Data
Names: Zappon, author. | Yasumo, illustrator. | DeLucia, Dale, translator.
Title: Banished from the hero's party, I decided to live a quiet life in the countryside / Zappon ; illustration by Yasumo ; translation by Dale DeLucia ; cover art by Yasumo.
Other titles: Shin no nakama ja nai to yuusha no party wo oidasareta node, henkyou de slow life suru koto ni shimashita. English
Description: First Yen On edition. | New York : Yen On, 2020.
Identifiers: LCCN 2020026847 | ISBN 9781975312459 (v. 1 ; trade paperback) |
ISBN 9781975312473 (v. 2 ; trade paperback) | ISBN 9781975312497 (v. 3 ; trade paperback) |
ISBN 9781975312510 (v. 4 ; trade paperback) | ISBN 9781975333423 (v. 5 ; trade paperback)
Subjects: CYAC: Ability—Fiction. | Fantasy.
Classification: LCC PZ7.1.Z37 Ban 2020 | DDC [Fic]—dc23
LC record available at https://lccn.loc.gov/2020026847

ISBNs: 978-1-9753-3342-3 (paperback)
978-1-9753-3343-0 (ebook)

1 3 5 7 9 10 8 6 4 2

LSC-C

CHARACTERS

Red
(Gideon Ragnason)

Kicked out of the Hero's party, he headed to the frontier to live a slow life. One of humanity's greatest swordsmen with many feats to his name.

Rit
(Rizlet of Loggervia)

The princess of the Duchy of Loggervia. Adventured with Red's party in the past. One thing led to another, and she forced herself into Red's shop and is now living with him. An easily embarrassed girl who has outgrown her more combative phase.

Ruti Ragnason

Red's younger sister and possessor of the Divine Blessing of the Hero, humanity's strongest blessing. Freed from her torturous blessing's impulses, she is enjoying her life in Zoltan with her beloved big brother.

Tisse Garland

A young girl with the Divine Blessing of the Assassin. She is Ruti's best friend, and they are currently starting a medicinal herb farm together. Her partner is a spider she named Mister Crawly Wawly.

Yarandrala

A high elf Singer of the Trees capable of controlling plants. One of the members of the Hero's party. She traveled in search of Red and has finally arrived in Zoltan.

Mistorm

An old lady with the Divine Blessing of the Archmage. A Zoltan hero with a broad range of experiences, from being mayor of Zoltan to being the leader of the previous generation's B-rank party.

Mogrim Bronzehead

A dwarf and self-proclaimed drake slayer. The neighborhood blacksmith who made Red's sword. He is truly devoted to his wife, Mink, a human he eloped with.

Godwin

An Alchemist who previously belonged to the Thieves Guild. He escaped Zoltan after Ruti let him go, but he was caught out on the road by Yarandrala.

▲ ▲

Prologue

- - - - - - - - -

Yaraŋdrala iŋ the (apital

▶ ▲ ▲ ◀ ◀

Ares, Ruti, and I were strolling along a road in the capital of Avalonia.

"What do we do next, Big Brother?" Ruti asked.

"The royal family has been informed of your blessing, and Ares's Appraisal has verified it. Coupled with my status as the second-in-command of the Bahamut Knights and the trust I've earned for my service to the crown, they're likely to accept who you are."

"I'm sure we'll be able to draw some minor monetary support with that," Ares added with a nod. "However, we'll need to be able to point to actual achievements to get the king to officially recognize you as the Hero. The Hero is a legendary blessing, so granting official recognition is a risk for the country."

"Before we came to the capital, we defeated and crushed a regiment of the demon lord's army that was attacking our hometown. That's certainly valiant, but not really something that only the Hero could have done," I remarked.

Ruti went quiet as she contemplated. "Then what is something that only the Hero could accomplish?" she asked.

"There's a band of thieves that has been active in the shadows here in the capital for the past fifty years," I responded. "A genuine criminal organization with no connection at all to the Thieves Guild."

"No one has done anything about them for that long?"

"Many people have tried. The guards, adventurers, even the Thieves Guild. Some attempts have gotten close, but none have successfully caught the mastermind, and the group has survived."

"I see."

While Ruti nodded along, Ares looked doubtful.

"Certainly, if we managed to take care of a band of ruffians that no one else has been able to destroy, that might be enough to be judged a feat worthy of the Hero, but do you have any leads for where to begin? With the demon lord's army closing in, time is not a luxury we can afford."

"I can't make any promises, but I do at least have a lead. The woman we're meeting with should be able to provide us the strength necessary to take care of them," I explained.

Ares frowned. "If there was someone who could do that, why have you just left the thieves alone until now?"

"Well, crimes inside the city are handled by the guards, not us Bahamut Knights..."

That excuse must have been unacceptable to Ares.

"Even so, you could have at least introduced her to the guards, couldn't you?"

"...At the lower levels it isn't that bad, but those in charge wouldn't trust a high elf."

"A high elf?! Can we really put our faith in a demi-human?"

"It's fine. High elves value trust more than contracts. That difference in conduct is probably why people with higher standings hate them. Besides, this band of thieves has been causing problems in the capital for fifty years now. There are other clues to be had, too, but on that alone, it's a fair bet the one in charge is a high elf as well. Thus we use a high elf to catch a high elf."

Leaving the road, we turned off into the small, wooded grove inside the walls of the capital. The air was still and quiet—a different world from the hustle and bustle of the streets.

"To think there's a place like this in the city," Ares remarked in wonder.

Ruti looked intrigued as she glanced around. We continued onward, surrounded by trees and birdsong.

"There's a house nearby, Big Brother."

Resting in a sunny spot was a brick cottage with a chimney. Beside it stood a large, stately, almost awe-inspiring Keyaki tree. As we drew near, the door swung open and a white blur leaped out from inside.

"Gideon!"

She hugged me and kissed my cheek. It was nothing more than a high elf greeting among friends, but I could sense Ruti's displeasure building behind me.

"I suppose introductions are in order. This is my friend Yarandrala," I said with a wry smile.

She glanced over my shoulder at Ares and Ruti and beamed.

"You're Ruti the Hero and Ares the Sage, right? I heard your discussion from my friends."

"Your friends?" Ares questioned, on guard.

Yarandrala released me and spread her hands wide.

"I'm Yarandrala, a Singer of the Trees. All plants are my friends!"

As if to emphasize her point, the forest around us seemed to sway.

Yarandrala was a reliable ally during our time in the capital, lending her strength to help track down and deal with the elusive band of thieves and to acquire the proof of the Hero. We parted ways when we left the city, but reunited during the battles in Loggervia, where she officially joined the party. We fought shoulder to shoulder through numerous battles until I was ousted from the party.

Chapter 1

Going to Get a Ring Made

On the continent of Avalon, there were just seven countries whose rulers were regarded as true kings. Thus this septet of nations was sometimes referred to as the seven kingdoms of Avalon.

There were other countries whose leaders were customarily addressed as kings, such as Loggervia. However, as implied by its name, the Duchy of Loggervia was not a true kingdom.

The largest of the seven was the Kingdom of Avalonia, Ruti and Red's home country. It was situated in the center of the continent and spanned the largest swath of territory.

The Flamberge Kingdom, a country of both the pen and the sword, sat on the west side of the continent and was destroyed battling the demon lord's army.

To the north lay the Kingdom of Kiramin, a giant city-state where the famed and proud high elves lived.

The Kingdom of Veronia controlled the southern coast. A pirate king named Geizeric had stolen the throne and raised the nation from destitution to the status of the second-greatest power in Avalon.

A knight-king descended from the previous Hero ruled the Cataphract Kingdom that controlled the northeastern plateau.

The Kingdom of Tian Long was a sizable land to the east that claimed dominion over all land beyond the Wall at the End of the World, guarded by the ancient lightning dragon.

Finally, there was the Jade Kingdom. A nation even farther to the east and separated from the dark continent by a channel. War had been raging there for many years.

Being regarded as an official kingdom did not necessarily denote power. The Duchy of Loggervia, a country with a proud military history and strong army, was far mightier than the Kingdom of Kiramin, with its limited territory, or the Kingdom of Veronia before Geizeric was crowned. However, the crown of each kingdom still wielded great influence over the lords and vassals.

It was rather ironic that those long-standing bloodlines were viewed as crucial to legitimizing rule to prevent people with blessings like Champion or Shogun from using their abilities to gather support.

When Red, Ruti, or the people of Zoltan referred to "the capital" or "Central," they meant the capital or central region of the Kingdom of Avalonia, respectively.

In an ideal world, all the kingdoms would unite to stand together against the demon invasion.

Unfortunately, Veronia had adopted an official stance of neutrality, limiting its support to a small number of volunteers who joined up with Avalonian forces. That opportunistic positioning drew derision from other nations, convincing many that a pirate was unfit to be a true king. Yet despite the criticisms, the ninety-year-old King Geizeric kept his silence.

Kiramin had proactively declared its intention to join the war against the demon lord's forces despite being far removed from the front line, but the differences between high elf and human thinking made effective cooperation difficult.

The Cataphract Kingdom's proud order of knights formed of its nomadic peoples had dispatched forces across the continent. They refused to take any orders from Avalonia, though, as it had been responsible for the destruction of Gaiapolis, the initial home of the Cataphract people, including the original ruler of central Avalon.

Those two countries to the east of the Wall at the End of the World possessed little knowledge of conditions on the front lines. Information came with traveling merchants who made it through the daybreak route. Recently, there had been rumors that the warriors of the Jade Kingdom were combating a powerful army sent by the demon lord. Regardless, Tian Long and the Jade Kingdom were beyond a perilous mountain range, so coordination with Avalonia was out of the question.

In the end, the various kingdoms fought against the demon lord's forces without unified leadership. Until the arrival of Ruti the Hero, they racked up loss after loss on crucial fronts, and for a time, the demon lord's army occupied a significant portion of the continent.

Ruti took back regions all across Avalon, and when the demon lord's most menacing threat, Gandor of the Wind's wyvern knight force, fell to her, things seemed to tip in the kingdoms' favor.

What's more, the Hero arranged a summit between the Cataphract Kingdom and the Kingdom of Avalonia where both sides made some minor concessions. For the time being, relations between the two had improved enough that both parties were willing to stand side by side on the battlefield.

Avalon's allied forces seemed poised to turn the tide, but the demon lord's army was not to be underestimated. The battle on the front lines quickly came to a stalemate, and reports reached Central that Vidosra, the new heavenly king of the wind, was re-forming the wyvern knights.

Avalonia was continuing its counteroffensive with the Bahamut Knights as the centerpiece of that push, but the outcome of the war was far from a foregone conclusion.

✱   ✱   ✱

"Oh, the price of vegetables is going up."

I was checking out produce in the Zoltan market. Green onions had recently only been five commons, yet now they were ten.

"Hmmm."

I had planned to cook with green onions, but the doubling in price gave me pause.

"Pardon me, why did green onions get so much more expensive all of a sudden?"

The old lady running the shop was bundled up in layers but still looked cold as she warmed her hands by a little charcoal heater. She sluggishly pulled herself away from it and hobbled over. The elderly woman stared at the green onions for a moment. I could almost feel a kind of silent determination, as though her eyes were pleading with me to just understand that some things couldn't be hel—

"Hmm, they got mislabeled."

"Oy!"

It was another peaceful day in Zoltan.

*   *   *

While I was walking around the marketplace, a familiar spider waved a front leg to me.

"Mister Crawly Wawly? By yourself today?"

I drew closer and held out my right hand, and he hopped up onto it. Then he shook his head back and forth.

"Hmm. You're concerned about something?"

After trying to communicate a few times, I somehow managed to discern the gist of what Mister Crawly Wawly was attempting to convey. I followed his directions, walking along the Zoltan streets.

For a spider, he was seriously high spec. He had recognized me and waved me over. Perhaps he had laid threads across the ground and realized who I was from my weight and gait as I strode across the strands.

After a bit, I spied a small figure wearing a hooded cloak sitting in front of a fruit stand and staring at the merchandise.

"I can promise you they're all delicious, miss, so please don't worry so much about it." With a troubled expression, a merchant held out an orange and asked, "How about this?"

The petite young woman, Tisse, gave it a quick glance before responding, "Please, don't mind me."

"Oh, if it isn't Red! Help me out here! This little lady has been here for over an hour."

"An hour?" I asked.

Mister Crawly Wawly waved his front legs as if to say he was concerned, too.

"Hey, Tisse, what's bothering you?"

"Ah, Red. Hello. It's nothing of importance," she responded in a completely serious tone. "It's just, isn't there a foreign custom of putting a citrus fruit into a bath?"

"Ahhh. I'm not particularly knowledgeable on the subject, but I do believe there is a country with a custom along those lines."

"It got me curious is the thing."

"And that's why you're here?"

"Yes, but I'm struggling to decide which fruit would be best to use."

"You've been grappling with that for more than an hour?"

Tisse had an aloof air to her, but on the inside, she was a kind person with a good head on her shoulders. However, the young woman was not without her own quirks.

"You were a member of that oddball party, too, Red," she reminded me.

"Oops, caught me, huh?"

Ruti, Danan, Theodora, Ares, Yarandrala, and Tisse. Compared to them, I counted myself as pretty harmless and bland.

"You are splendidly eccentric, too," Tisse added.

"I'll take your word for it."

Mister Crawly Wawly averted his eyes, as if to indicate he was normal, unlike us.

"W-well, setting that aside…I don't really know the actual custom, but…most likely any citrus fruit would work to create a nice scent for a bath," I stated.

Tisse nodded thoughtfully. "I see. Which would you go with?"

"Hmmm, I imagine mikan or yuzu might be pretty good."

"Mikan and yuzu? Yeah, those would be good to try."

"You've finally decided?! Thank goodness."

The merchant looked relieved. He managed to sell me some mikan, too.

✳   ✳   ✳

Tisse and I were both walking back with bags in hand.

"By the way, where did the sudden curiosity about that foreign custom come from?" I asked.

"Yesterday, I took on a job rescuing some villagers and adventurers who had been captured by trolls, and this older woman who was a mage and retired adventurer helped out."

"Oh? Someone capable enough to actually support you?"

"There were two entrances, so I had her wait at one while I went in from the other. She took out all of the trolls who tried to escape by herself."

"Wow, that's something you don't see every day."

"Indeed. So after it was over, she happened to comment that she'd like to relax with a nice soak, which sparked a pleasant conversation about baths."

"You two struck up a rapport?"

Tisse generally kept a straight face and was very businesslike, so getting a real conversation out of her on a first encounter wasn't easy. That woman had to be pretty capable.

"Anyway, I heard about the citrus custom from her, but unfortunately, I couldn't recall which fruits she mentioned, which is how I ended up here."

"Looking to test it the very next day after you heard about it? You really love your baths."

"I do."

"Uh-huh."

No hesitation at all. Curiously, Tisse seemed smug about it.

"Uhhh, then how would you feel about all of us going to a hot spring sometime?" I suggested.

"Is there such a place nearby?"

"I feel like I've heard a rumor of one near the Wall at the End of the World."

"A natural hot spring? Fascinating."

Tisse's eyes were sparkling.

What was I going to do now if it was only a myth?

"Oh yeah," I began, abruptly changing the subject. "Does that woman live in town?"

"No, I think she resides in a slightly isolated settlement but happened to be around visiting some friends in Zoltan. So when were you planning to visit this hot spring?"

"I-I'll look into a date that's convenient for all of us."

Tisse wasn't going to let it go, so I didn't have any other choice...

✳   ✳   ✳

Tisse and I split up after finishing our grocery shopping. While walking back home, I heard cheers from a nearby field.

"Whoaaaaa!"

"That's five wins in a row!"

"She's the wyvern queen!"

What's that? Curious, I detoured a bit to check out what the fuss was about.

"You're amazing!!!"

"Heh-heh!"

It was Ruti. She was playing the board game wyvern race with a bunch of children. Judging by her big smile, she was really enjoying herself.

Evidently, she was on a bit of a winning streak and had captured a bunch of the children's wyvern figures.

"R-rematch! I want a rematch!" demanded one child.

"Sure."

Ruti placed a glass wyvern figure on the board. Its sparkling construction was a marvel to behold. Undaunted, the children set up a white stone wyvern, a black steel one, and a red-eyed one.

A figure's quality did not provide any real advantage, but as Zoltan played by winner-take-all rules, unique miniatures exerted a kind of psychological pressure because of the confidence one needed to risk losing them. The game could be played with wyverns scribbled on bits of wood or some pebbles, but being willing to match your best wyvern against your opponent's was a way to mentally keep yourself on an equal footing, and it was a key trick for success.

"Looks like things are heating up here."

"Big Brother?!"

Noticing me, Ruti looked flustered, like a little kid caught fooling around with something she wasn't supposed to. Her reaction was so adorable that I couldn't help smiling.

"That's a pretty amazing collection. You must have been winning a lot."

"Uh—ummm…"

"You always wanted to try playing, right? There's nothing wrong with that."

Ruti had been the Hero since she was a child. Consequently, making friends had been very difficult for her. She'd never been part of the group of children in our village.

To the best of my knowledge, she hadn't ever played wyvern race before. But I did know that over the course of our journey, she had been gathering wyvern figures when she could get her hands on them without drawing attention.

Ruti looked a bit ashamed at being caught taking wyverns from children, but that was the wrong way to look at it. Whether you were playing against children or adults, the thrill of wyvern race was in betting your figures on the roll of the dice. There was no shame in her collecting the wagered miniatures if she won.

I flashed a reassuring smile so Ruti wouldn't be worried.

"I played it a bit myself back when I was an apprentice with the knights."

"You did?"

"We can all play together sometime if you want."

"Okay." Ruti nodded happily.

There was a charcoal heater near my feet as I sat at the counter and looked through my notes with a groan. It had been a day since my run-ins with Ruti and Tisse.

"A gemstone..."

I was struggling with what to do about the jewel for Rit's ring. She had said that she would be happy with whatever I chose, but that was why I wanted to find the perfect stone for her.

Setting the question of funds aside, there weren't a lot of gems to be found out here in the boonies.

Zoltan butted right up against the Wall at the End of the World, making it a dead end of sorts. Thus, only things in real demand made it here. And when it came to jewels, the selection was the bare minimum of those suited to the local aristocrats. Wealthy people around here tended to be more particular about fabrics than gems. They found colorful, multilayered outfits more appealing because that was the style in Central. Accessories were relegated to an afterthought. Such attire was widely panned by the Zoltan working class. It was hot and suffocating just to look at them.

"...I really don't want to concede on this, though. A pale-blue sapphire would suit her eyes best."

I crossed off all the gemstones on the compromise list.

"Okay, I guess I'll have to go to the Wall at the End of the World."

If you wanted to find precious stones near Zoltan, the giant mountain range dividing the continent was your only choice. The gem giants living there would have most any jewel.

However, I had come to Zoltan to take it easy and live a slow life, so I hadn't investigated the lay of the land around the mountain range.

I unfurled a map made by a local cartographer, but it was mostly blank. There was a wide swath of unexplored land. I traced a big circle in the uncharted space with my finger.

"Their settlement should be somewhere in here... That's really too wide a range, though."

Were I planning to gather people and supplies for a months-long exploratory expedition, it would be a different story, but I obviously wasn't. I didn't have the funds for such a venture.

"I should visit the zoog village first."

There was a village of rodent-like monsters called zoogs near the base of the mountain range that formed the Wall at the End of the World. Zoogs possessed human-level intelligence, so hopefully they would know a fair bit about the surroundings. They were not particularly friendly to outsiders, but I had rescued a young wounded zoog and returned it to its village a while back, so I was on good enough terms with them. They would welcome me if I brought along some meat as a gift.

"Red, I've finished the job."

"Thank you."

Rit was back from the delivery to Dr. Newman's clinic. She slipped her gloves off, removed her coat, and headed over to me. Her cheeks were red from the winter cold, so I cupped my hands over them.

"Your hands are so warm."

Lately, we had gotten in the habit of doing things like this after one of us went outside for something.

"I've got a heater here, so let's warm up together."

"Mm, in that case..."

Rit slightly adjusted my hands on her cheeks to hide the fact that she was starting to blush a bit and break into a smile as she sat down beside me.

"Eh-heh-heh."

Then she wrapped her cold legs around one of mine.

"Wh-whoa, wait a sec, Rit."

"You can use the heater, and I'll just take your warmth."

Rit's thighs squeezed tight. Her legs were chilly from walking around outside, but my face and body were only getting hotter.

"You're blushing, Red."

"...You're beet red, too."

"That's just from walking around outside," Rit teased.

I could feel her grinning behind my hands. As payback for her remark, I kneaded her cheeks a bit.

Today was a good day.

Once she wasn't so cold, Rit moved away a bit and looked at the map spread out on the counter.

"Huh? Why did you have that out?"

"Ah, that's, well..."

"Spit it out already... Wait!" Rit latched on to me all of a sudden. "You're thinking about going off on an adventure by yourself, aren't you?"

"You've got it all wrong..." I wasn't trying to keep it a secret, but explaining my intentions was kind of embarrassing. "I'm just planning out how to get a gem for your ring."

"Ah..." Rit's expression softened before my eyes. "Th-that's right... the gem for the ring..."

She pressed her forehead into my chest and squeezed me tight to conceal her flushed face.

"Eh-heh-heh, the ring..."

Rit's shoulders trembled in my arms. Her reaction was just so endearing that I had to kiss her forehead.

$$* \qquad * \qquad *$$

The two of us held each other like that until we heard a customer enter and hurriedly broke away. The half-elf carpenter Gonz had come in and was smirking as Rit and I disentangled ourselves. After he purchased the medicine he needed and left, we pulled the map back out from under the counter to look over it again.

"All right, where were you going to get the gemstone?" Rit inquired.

"There's a village of gem giants up in the Wall at the End of the World, and I was hoping they might sell me one."

"What?!"

Seeing her surprise, I explained my plan a bit more.

"I see…but it's not like you have to go that far for me. I would treasure anything you chose for me, even if it was a common stone."

"You told me to pick out a ring for you, and I don't want to make any compromises. It's a once-in-a-lifetime ring for me, too, after all."

"Once in a lifetime…eh-heh-heh…," giggled Rit with an uncomposed grin. After hiding behind her red bandana in embarrassment, she nodded. "Okay, I understand. If you're going to put that much love into it, then I'll be sure to accept it with at least that much affection, too! I can't wait to see what kind of ring you'll get for me!"

"Leave it to me. That said, I don't really know if I'll be able to find the gem giants. And if I do, who can say if they have what I'm looking for…? If this doesn't work, I have some blue agate on hold with a merchant. Hopefully it doesn't come to that. It'd be quite the disappointment."

"You're wrong! There's no way I could be disappointed after learning how hard you're trying! There's no one in the world cooler than my Red!" Rit exclaimed. Her tone made it obvious she meant every word.

I hid my reddening cheeks and slack-jawed smirk behind my right arm as I considered starting to wear a bandana around my neck like Rit.

Seeing me blushing, Rit pressed her lips together as if trying to hold something back.

"Aaargh! You're the best! You better take responsibility if I end up loving you even more than I already do!"

Rit wrapped her arms around me and kissed me.

*   *   *

Again, a customer arrived, and we swiftly distanced ourselves.

This time, the local dwarf blacksmith stepped in, paying no heed to what we had obviously been doing. He strode over to the counter and dropped his arms down on it with a thud.

"Red! It's a good day, isn't it!"

"It sure is, Mogrim. So what can I do for you? I doubt a dwarf like you is looking for a hangover cure."

Mogrim's bearded face split in a wide grin.

"Damn straight! Any dwarf from Sir Beard Mountain can swallow a drake's skull filled to the brim with whiskey and get up the next morning to stoke the furnace without missing a beat. I swear on my ax!"

Loving booze was a dwarf's pride. When imbibing with a dwarf, it was important to state that you would drink at your own pace. Dwarves understood that consuming alcohol was a status symbol only among their kind, and the vast majority wouldn't force the case with someone from another race who turned down a drink.

Some would go on about how "no-beards are all just a bunch of kids who can't handle a little sip!" and make a show of dominance about it, but there were jerks everywhere.

Mogrim was a laid-back sort of guy, a bit of an outlier among his people. He didn't pressure others.

"Say, did I ever tell you the story of the deadly orochi drake that came from the Far East and how I managed to get it drunk and slay it?"

This self-proclaimed drake slayer's only major flaw was his tendency toward recounting tall tales of his supposed feats.

"You may have mentioned it. So what medicine were you wanting?" I asked.

"Oh yeah, that. I've got a good friend coming over tonight. I was hoping you could share a bit of your spices."

"Spices, huh? Sure. I owe you for your help with the ingredients for the warmers, after all."

"Great! I'll be sure to pay you back for this!"

I gathered up the seasonings Mogrim wanted in several little bags and handed them over. He gripped my hand in a big handshake and thanked me in a loud voice before purchasing a few nutritional cookies and departing.

The shop fell silent again as Rit and I smiled at each other.

"So when are you going?"

"To the Wall? Honestly, there's not much time left until the night of the solstice festival, and that's when I wanted it all ready. Actually, I was planning to leave the day after tomorrow."

"So soon! Okay, I'll get my things in order, too, then!"

"Huh?"

"Obviously, I'm coming with you."

"Er, but I'm going to get a gemstone for you, so getting your help is sort of...," I protested.

"There's nothing wrong with that! The important part is that you choose the stone for me. It's fine for us to share the load when it comes to actually acquiring it!" Rit declared, her sky-blue eyes trained on mine.

"...I guess so. Sorry. We can make the trip together."

"Yeah!"

That meant taking some more time to prepare more appealing travel rations.

Even the notion of exploring the Wall at the End of the World sounded fun when I imagined doing it with Rit.

$$* \qquad * \qquad *$$

Ruti and Tisse came over for dinner. Tonight's menu was a potato soup and chicken thighs sautéed in butter.

"Delicious."

Ruti enjoyed the meal with great enthusiasm.

After we had all finished, I said, "Ruti."

"What is it?"

"There's something I wanted to talk about."

The trip to the Wall would keep me away from Zoltan for a while. There was no way I couldn't tell my sister.

"I'm planning to head out to the Wall at the End of the World in two days."

"Why there?"

"I'm going to a village of gem giants to trade some glass for a gemstone. Which means I won't be home for some time."

"Okay." Ruti nodded as she stared directly at me. "I'll go, too."

"Umm…"

There was a clarity to Ruti's voice that made her sound all the more forceful.

"I've been waiting for this moment," she stated.

"You have?"

"I've been on more adventures and gone through more fights than I can count, but all because I was the Hero. And you faced those dangers for my sake. I'm really grateful for all of that," Ruti explained, her gaze on me unwavering. "But I've never once done the same for you. I've never fought for you. I want to support you using the strength that I have."

Ruti paused to lean in close.

"Please let me go with you, Big Brother."

"I—I see. Heh. I never knew you felt that way. Thank you. It's nice to know that. And I understand better than anyone how reliable you are. It would be reassuring to have you with me."

"Okay."

Ruti clenched her fists, determined to help. So cute.

With slight nervousness, I asked, "Umm, what about you, Tisse?"

"I'll watch the shop and continue preparations for the herb farm. The three of you shouldn't have any issue with monsters."

Tisse beamed as she beheld Ruti's determination. My younger sister had truly found a great friend.

"By the way."

"Hmm?"

"What is the gemstone for, Big Brother?"

A chill fell over the room. Tisse froze, and Rit and I glanced at each other. Ruti seemingly didn't notice, her expression unclouded. I took a deep breath before slowly responding.

"I'm planning to get an engagement ring made."

Tisse gave an audible gulp. Rit looked nervous as she clasped her hands together.

"Big Brother." Ruti looked up at me with her red eyes. "Congratulations. That's great."

She looked pleased as she smiled.

*   *   *

"Whew, I was nervous there," admitted Rit after Ruti and Tisse had left. Her arms relaxed, and she laughed nervously. "I'm surprised, though. She's really attached to you. I thought she might be upset about having her big brother taken."

"Yeah. The reason she couldn't really develop any affection toward other people was because of her blessing, though. Without that holding her back, maybe she's found someone else besides me."

The Divine Blessing of the Hero came with psychological resistances and immunities that had prevented Ruti from developing typical human affections toward other people. The memory of her feelings for me from before gaining those was the only love that she had been able to experience.

Now, thanks to New Truth, she was able to turn her immunities on and off as she pleased. She could fall in love with whomever she liked.

"She's growing up and doesn't need her big brother anymore. It's a little bittersweet, honestly," I confessed.

"You do love to dote on her," Rit remarked.

"Mrgh…I won't deny it."

"What'll you do if she ends up with someone like Godwin?"

"Assassinate him."

"Th-that's not something you should say with a straight face. It doesn't sound like a joke when you put it like that."

I had meant it in jest...though if the time ever did come, would I really be able to stay levelheaded? If Ruti truly loved someone like that, I wasn't sure I'd have a choice.

"Silly Red."

Rit smiled wryly, as if she had realized what I was thinking.

✳   ✳   ✳

It has always been clear they were headed that way, but after that conversation...

My name is Tisse Garland. An Assassin and the love-stricken Hero's best friend.

Moments before, Ruti had congratulated Red on his engagement to Rit. At a glance, it seemed like she had given up on her brother and was offering the two her best wishes for their shared future. Red and Rit might have taken it to mean that Ruti had moved on.

However, they were wrong. After spending so much time with Ruti, I could tell.

"Ms. Ruti, is this okay?"

"Is what okay?"

"Red and Rit."

"Oh." Ruti nodded. "Rit's a good person. I'm sure she will cherish Big Brother. Recently, I've even started to think that if anyone was going to be Big Brother's wife, she would be a good fit."

"Is that so? That's all fine...but aren't you going to feel lonely if he gets married?"

"Lonely? Why?"

"Umm..."

Ruti smiled at me. It was a clear expression bearing no ill will.

"I can't marry Big Brother, since we're siblings. So I'll let Rit be his wife."

"Uh, umm?"

"Even if we're not wedded, we can still be lovers."

Ruti's doll-like, almost expressionless face turned ever so slightly red.

"Big Brother's very broad-minded, so he can handle two people just fine. Rit can be his spouse, but we can be a couple, too."

"…"

Red, you've gravely misunderstood the situation. It's true that Ruti develops feelings for others now, but affection doesn't just go up equally for everyone. Now that she's unrestrained, her love for you is growing greater every day. She might well be past a point of no return.

Mister Crawly Wawly on my shoulder and I both tilted our heads, wondering what we could do about this.

*   *   *

There was a small village not far off the road that travelers often stopped at on their way to Zoltan.

If more people ventured this way, the settlement might have grown to be a tavern town, but few bothered to make the trip to Zoltan. Thus, despite this village being a day's journey from Zoltan, it had only a single two-story inn.

A beautiful high elf and a dejected man were sitting at a dirty table outside the tavern. The worn-down chair legs were not all the same height, so their occupants wobbled back and forth. The dejected man scratched his face while chewing on a pickled carrot.

"Hey. I told you where they live, so you don't need me anymore, right?" the man asked in a nervous, hushed tone.

"I don't know whether you've told me the truth yet. And you seem like a criminal, so I can't just let you roam free," Yarandrala fired back immediately.

She didn't even pretend to care about her associate's reproachful look.

"You said you'd let me go if I talked!" the man protested.

"I only asked if you would answer my question. I never said word one about doing anything for you if you cooperated."

"Cut me some slack here!"

The man clawed at his face again.

"If you keep scratching like that, your face will slip off," chided Yarandrala.

"But it really stings."

"The fungus is growing into your flesh, so that's to be expected."

"Is this really okay? Will it take my skin with it when it comes off?"

"You'll be fine. It will take care of all of your acne and leave you with a nice, smooth face afterward. If anything, the fungus is complaining about how unclean your skin is. You need to learn to wash your face properly."

"Th-the fungus is complaining?"

Anyone who saw him now wouldn't recognize the man, but he was Godwin the Alchemist. Previously, he'd been Bighawk's right-hand man and the member of the Thieves Guild who had prepared Devil's Blessing and kidnapped the half-elf boy Al. After Godwin was jailed for his crimes, Ruti had broken him out. From there, he'd been embroiled in the fight against Ares.

Yarandrala had spread a fungus called yellow mask across Godwin's face. Yellow mask created a new appearance and voice when applied. It was an incredibly dangerous fungus that could parasitize a person's nervous system, even control their movements, if allowed to spread to the back of one's head. However, with Yarandrala's ability to manipulate plants, it was not doing anything more than altering Godwin's appearance and speech.

If Godwin had known yellow mask's true nature, he would have undoubtedly made a big fuss, but fortunately, he'd trusted Yarandrala's explanation that it was merely used for disguises.

"Very much so, yes." Seeing Godwin sulking, Yarandrala lowered her voice a bit. "For someone who claimed to be Rit's friend, you were awfully quick to reveal where she was living."

"You said that you didn't come to cause any problems for Rit and Red."

"And you took me at my word. If you truly were their companion, shouldn't you have probed more and made sure I wasn't an enemy?"

"Look, I told you what I know like you asked, so why are you scolding me? High elves really are a pain in the ass!"

"It's because humans trust others far too readily."

Godwin heaved a sigh. Evidently, he had no choice but to return to Zoltan with Yarandrala. If the guards somehow managed to see through his disguise, it would be the end of the line for him.

Even if I try to run, this Yarandrala or whatever is crazy strong. I don't see how I could escape... The only way out is to hope Red and the others can get her to release me.

They had let him go once before, after all. Godwin's only hope was that they would explain things to this high elf.

✳   ✳   ✳

Come afternoon the next day, I was carrying a big bag on my back as I perused the market.

"What else do I need to get...?"

My first extended trip into the wilderness in a long while was fast approaching, and I was gathering miscellaneous bits and pieces I would need.

"I've got a charcoal heater and some flint. We can just use fallen branches for firewood, but I've got one day's worth to be safe. Thirty meters of silk rope, a new tent, an old blanket, a jar of oil for the lantern, three bars of soap, ten pieces of chalk, a dozen torches, a whetstone, waterproof bags, a pot, a ladle, skewers, a cutting board, a tripod for the pot. It's a nice one that you can attach the skewers to for grilling. And I've got the pork to give the zoogs and glass marbles for the gem giants."

The expenses for the preparations hurt a bit, but if I could get the gem giants to trade me any extra jewels, I'd be able to make up what I'd lost without much trouble. Dealing in gemstones wasn't really an apothecary's job, but if I was already there and could make something out of it, I might as well.

"Should I go with fourteen days of rations to be on the safe side? … Yeah, and I think I'll make some elven preserves this time."

I thought back to a recipe that my old friend Yarandrala had taught me.

It was for a soft bread kneaded with sugar and milk. Typically, something like that wouldn't keep for very long, but the high elves had worked out a preservation method whereby they made a paste using fay strawberries and brownberries and then coated the bread in it. With that, the bread could last for half a year without going bad.

Danan and the others had liked it quite a bit, though honestly it seemed Danan would say anything was tasty. Either way, a sugary bread would be good for a tired body.

"I've got most of the ingredients already, but I need to make sure to pick up some fay strawberries."

Despite my carrying a large bag, my footsteps felt lighter as I imagined Rit's expression when she ate the bread.

*   *   *

Night fell, and Rit and I had closed up shop and were getting ready for tomorrow.

"There, that should be perfect for this!"

"What? Oooh, that's a knife from Igosu, isn't it?"

"Light and sturdy. And it's magic, too. Look, you can freeze it floating in the air. You can hook bags and tents on it."

"Nice, that looks pretty handy."

The two of us were taking our time packing, and Rit was having fun showing off the convenient gear she was bringing.

We weren't exactly making incredible progress, but that was all right. Even if we didn't complete things tonight, we could finish in the morning and set out by noon, or even the next day, if necessary. This adventure was just one more aspect of our slow life. Making it a fun journey was more important to us than efficiency.

Just as I was thinking as much, trouble did wind up coming to call.

"Red! Sorry, but can you please let me in?!"

Mogrim was knocking on the door, and his voice was hoarse.

"What's wrong?" I asked.

Sensing something was up, Rit and I immediately went out to the storefront. After opening the door, I saw that Mogrim was standing there barefoot, his face red from exertion beneath his beard.

"Red! The missus collapsed!"

"What?!"

"Dr. Newman came to see her but said he didn't have enough medicine! He told me it would be faster to just come to you instead of going to the clinic and back. Here, look at this. It's got everything written on it."

I took the doctor's note Mogrim offered and read it over.

"...These are for anemia and dehydration."

"Really? I don't really know what it's all about, but you can get them for her, right?"

"And there's one other medicine listed for her to take later if she needs it." I looked the dwarf straight in the eyes. "Mogrim, what did Dr. Newman tell you before you came here?"

"I'm pretty sure he mentioned a lot of things, but I just sort of lost my head when the missus collapsed, and only got the bit about her needing medicine... Wh-why? Is it something really bad?"

"What is it, Red?" Rit sounded worried as she peeked over my shoulder at the note. "Ah! That's..." She noticed it, too. "Congratulations, Mogrim!"

"What?! My wife collapsed and you're congratulating me?!"

"The last two medicines on the list are cold and headache medicine for women who are expecting."

"Huh?"

"Mink is pregnant," I stated.

Mogrim stood there flabbergasted for a moment before covering his mouth with both hands. In response, I hurriedly covered my ears.

"Yaaahoooooooo!!!"

People joked that a dwarven victory cry could knock even an orc hussar off their horse. Upon hearing Mogrim, I finally understood.

*　　　　　*　　　　　*

I left the preparations for tomorrow to Rit and went with Mogrim to deliver the medicine. Dr. Newman and an older human woman were already at Mogrim's workshop.

Oh yeah, he mentioned he had a guest coming the other day. I guess this is she.

"Oh, Red, you're here already?"

"I brought the medicine you asked for."

"Ha-ha, it wasn't a big rush or anything. Still, Mogrim was insistent I check up on Mink," explained Dr. Newman.

"How is she?" I asked.

"Merely a little anemic. She was only unconscious for a very short time. I imagine she's built up a lot of fatigue the past few days. It's likely she'll need to cut back on her work hours going forward. There don't seem to be any issues for either the mother or child, however."

"So she really is pregnant."

"Yes, about three months along."

Mogrim was already winding up for another shout, but I frantically covered his mouth.

"You'll disturb Mink!" I scolded him.

Mogrim's eyes went wide, and he nodded.

"Ooooh." Tears were streaming from the dwarf's eyes as he struggled to keep his voice down. "I thought I was too old to be having kids."

"I'm sure Kyutie, the guardian of love, bestowed a blessing on your harmonious marriage," the old lady remarked as she patted Mogrim's back. Then she turned to me with a slight smile. "I don't believe we've met. Is that right? At my age, it gets a bit hard to remember."

"Yes, it's nice to meet you, ma'am. My name is Red. I moved to Zoltan last year and am running an apothecary nearby."

"Oh, so you're that Red? I've heard all sorts of stories about you. It's nice to finally make your acquaintance."

She looked me up and down and then nodded.

"And the rumors didn't lie. You are quite the handsome young fellow. Also, please, you don't need to be so formal with me just because I'm old. I'm just a retired lady."

"Okay. By the way, what sort of rumors have you heard, Ms., umm..."

"Oops, I never gave you my name, did I?"

I examined her a bit closer. She looked to be in her seventies. Despite her walking stick, she seemed as steady on her legs as any. There were vestiges of what had probably been a beautiful face beneath the wrinkles, and her black eyes still held a lively energy. Her hair was snow white. While her robe sported no adornments, it was woven with silver silkworm thread, making it quite valuable. The material was durable, enough to endure decades of travel.

"My name is Mistorm. I used to be the mayor a long time ago."

She stopped patting Mogrim's back and held out her hand. When I took it and shook, her grip was far stronger than I'd expected.

"Ms. Mistorm...so you're Master Mistorm."

"You can skip all that 'master' business."

The title of master was granted to members of the Mages Guild who had accomplished some special achievement or provided distinguished service. I had heard that Mistorm had been chosen to be the mayor of Zoltan after having served as the head of the Mages Guild and that she had been granted her mastership after finishing her term running the town.

"All I ever did was handle the work others gave me. I never did anything that special as head of the guild or mayor. It's embarrassing to be called master."

"In that case, I'll stick to just Mistorm."

"That'd be just fine."

I watched the old woman's face as she smiled, but there did not seem to be any hidden intent. The sort of politicians who rose to steward cities weren't above putting on a friendly guise in order to gauge how much respect someone really had for them, but Mistorm seemed to genuinely desire a relationship on a more equal footing.

"Would it be okay for me to say hi to Mink, too?" I asked Dr. Newman.

"Of course. I'm sure she'll be happy for the company."

Hearing that, Mogrim bounded off.

"Mink!!!"

He dashed to the bedroom on his short legs.

The door slammed open, followed by a voice that resounded throughout the neighborhood:

"Thank you, Mink! You did it!"

To which Mink heartily fired back, "I'm pretty sure you're the one who did the doing!"

And then I could hear the two of them tearing up in hushed, affectionate tones.

"Maybe I should leave them alone for a bit," I said.

"That might be a good idea," Mistorm responded.

*   *   *

After a bit, I finally popped my head in to say hello and then headed back home.

Mink seemed annoyed at being treated like she was sick, but Mogrim was insistent that she rest. He even bravely stepped up to take care of the washing and cleaning that Mink normally did, though with a healthy helping of muttered complaints, and only after Mink had given him a kick to get him to work.

Mogrim must have been really happy.

Rit was tickled imagining the scene as I explained what had

happened. "Mink definitely runs their home, but Mogrim really is devoted to her."

"I mean, he did leave the dwarf country to elope with her. There's no mistaking how much he loves his wife. And he was so happy he cried when he realized they were going to have a child," I replied.

"A child. It must be nice."

"We'll have to do our best, too…"

"Eh-heh-heh. Mm-hmm."

Rit hugged me softly. I held her gently, basking in her warmth as I imagined our future.

I was sure it was going to be lovely.

"Red."

"What?"

"I really love the way your face looks right now," Rit responded with a delighted smile.

I could feel my cheeks burning, but I didn't try to hide it. I just pressed my forehead to hers and grinned back, still blushing.

"A-anyway, how are the preparations for tomorrow? If they're not done yet, we can just delay it a day."

"It's fine. I finished everything."

"Dependable as always. Thank you."

"I mean, you're going on an adventure for me, after all. Eh-heh-heh. I'm so happy."

Mogrim and Mink were really close with each other, but Rit and I weren't about to lose to them.

And as that thought crossed my mind, I hugged Rit just a little bit tighter.

Chapter 2

Companions for the Road

It was still a bit dark out, so most of the residents of Zoltan, always loath to get up early, were probably still asleep. Still, it wasn't like it was *that* early. It was just dark because of the season.

"All right! Everything's ready to go!" Rit said.

The bigger things like tents were safely tucked away in Rit's item box, and I was carrying the objects we might need to use more immediately, like the lantern and a few days' worth of food and water in case the item box got stolen.

I had also pulled out a wide variety of medicines from storage that Rit and I had tucked away into pouches at our belts.

"All right, shall we?"

Just then, there was a loud knocking at the door. "Red! It's me! Sorry to come so early, but can you let me in?"

"Mogrim? Did something else happen?"

The dwarf had come knocking again. We were supposed to be closed for the day, but if Mink needed some medicine, I could take care of that before leaving.

However, when I opened the door, Mogrim was standing there wearing chain mail and with a dwarven ax at his hip. A large bag was on his back.

It sure didn't look like he was just out to buy medicine.

"What's with that outfit? Are you heading out on a trip somewhere?"

"I could ask you the same thing. You look ready for an adventure! But whatever. Red! Can you loan me some medicines?"

"Just a minute. Could you tell me what's going on?"

"Of course. I'm planning to go to the Wall at the End of the World."

"Why…? Shouldn't you be with Mink?"

Mogrim's expression suddenly turned very serious.

"The missus turned forty-five last year. She's not a young lass anymore. Half-dwarves tend to have smaller bodies and are easier to give birth to, but… You understand what I mean, right?"

"I see. Dr. Newman's specialty isn't obstetrics, so it would be a good idea to have the midwife Ivana come by to check on Mink, too. She has the Healer blessing and a wealth of experience, so I'm sure she'll be able to help."

"It might end up coming down to surgery and taking the child out through her belly, though."

"A surgical delivery? I can't deny the possibility, but even if it comes to that, the odds of failure are pretty low, so long as you can get someone reasonably skilled with restorative magic," I said.

"I want to do everything I can for her, but I don't have any talent for magic, and my blessing hates me. I don't have any skills that can help Mink in any direct way."

Mogrim was the best blacksmith in Zoltan's working-class neighborhood, but his blessing was Runesmith, one that specialized in magical enhancements. He had never used it very well because of his difficulties with magic. Given his talent for forging, if he were more proficient with magic, he could become a famed craftsman in the capital. Hence the comment about being hated by his blessing.

Mogrim clenched his fists in determination as he continued.

"All I'm good at is hammering. That's why I want to make a knife out of earth crystal. Earth crystal blades are famous for being so sharp you don't even realize you've been cut. If it really does come down to a surgery, that should ease Mink's burden."

"Earth crystal? That's a pretty rare material. You're not going to find that just lying around in Zoltan," I remarked.

"Yep. That's why I'm going out to the Wall. It's a special kind of gem to monsters, too, so I'm sure there's a creature out there that has gathered some of it."

"True, there are gem giants there. If there is any earth crystal to be found at the Wall, they would probably have gathered some of it."

"Oooh! So there really are gem giants there?! That's great!" Mogrim grinned happily. However, even knowing about the gem giants, he had no idea where they were or what to trade for the earth crystal.

What's more...

"Did you tell Mink that you were going?" I questioned.

"...Of course..."

"Look me in the eye and say that."

Unlike humans and high elves, dwarves were typically not talented liars, and Mogrim was the archetypal example. He was clearly avoiding my eyes.

"I told her that I was going to get materials to make a knife!"

"Where exactly did you say you were going?" I pressed.

"...The mountain city Zkaria."

Zkaria was a town to the northwest that was known for quality iron. It also offered small amounts of rare ores like crimson steel. There was no earth crystal to be found there, however.

"But! Who do you think I am?! Did I ever tell you about the time I slew the frost drake that was menacing the powerful Duchy of Loggervia?!"

Glancing over at Rit, I saw her smiling wryly as she shook her head. Apparently, Mogrim had slain a dragon that even the princess of Loggervia hadn't heard of. Mogrim stomped his foot and expounded on his vague tale as I nodded along to pacify the man.

"I've got a bit of a proposal if you're interested. It just so happens that Rit and I were planning on heading to the Wall at the End of the World ourselves."

"What? It did look like you were decked out for a trip, but..."

"The truth is...we're going to get a gemstone to use for a ring," I admitted.

Mogrim went agape as he looked back and forth between us.

"I thought *I* was a bit extreme, but you two are on a whole other level!" The dwarf clapped his hands together and made a show of being taken aback. "My word! Going all the way out there to make an engagement ring!"

"Anyway, that's our plan. So how about it? Want to go together? I'm just a D rank, but with the one and only Rit the hero, we'll be fine even if a real drake shows up."

"I swear on my ax! You two are lifesavers!" Mogrim responded with dwarflike boisterous joy as he grabbed our hands. "You have my thanks!"

"Save the thanks for after you get your earth crystal. But you need to understand something up front, Mogrim."

"What?"

"Even if we locate the gem giants, there's no guarantee they'll have any earth crystal. And if they do, it's not likely you'll be able to convince them to part with it. You should consider what to do if you need to compromise on some other ore," I warned him earnestly.

Gem giants were skilled at mining and crafting precious metals and stones, but they had not developed any skills for using fire. To them, glass marbles were far more valuable than silver coins were for humans. With luck, glass could even be traded for diamonds. Earth crystal was another matter, though. It was unlikely the gem giants would give it up. Mogrim seemed aware of that.

"Even so. I want to do whatever I can for my wife," he stated as he looked down.

✳   ✳   ✳

The three of us headed toward the plaza near the gate.

Ruti was waiting there with a large backpack. Tisse was by her side, dressed as she usually was.

"Good morning, Ruti, Tisse. Sorry for being late," I called.

"It's fine. I don't mind waiting for you. Good morning, Big Brother, Rit…and Mogrim?"

"Good morning, everyone," Tisse greeted us. "It doesn't seem like you're here just to see them off, Mogrim."

Mister Crawly Wawly was on Tisse's shoulder, still sleepily swaying a bit.

"It's a bit sudden, but Mogrim will be coming with us. He's looking to find some earth crystal," I explained.

"I see." Ruti looked slightly surprised. Not so much so that Mogrim would notice, though. My sister recognized that earth crystal would be difficult to obtain.

"I see, so that's how it is," Tisse said after hearing the story from Rit. "Congratulations, Mogrim. I sincerely hope you will be careful. I don't doubt your dwarven bravery, but please remember that there is no greater honor than returning home safely to Mink and being able to raise your healthy child together with her."

"A-aye. I've never really had a chance to talk much with you, but you're a surprisingly nice person."

"That 'surprisingly' is a bit rude."

"Tisse is a very good person. I'm proud to call her my friend."

Although Tisse kept a calm face, she still seemed rather annoyed as Ruti expressionlessly puffed out her chest and bragged about her friend. The whole scene was a bit perplexing for Mogrim, but realizing that the two of them were not as intense as he had believed, he smiled back with the sort of smile dwarves reserved for friends.

"By the way, Ruti, were you not going to use your item box?" I inquired.

"No. Just like you."

Apparently, she was emulating me on that point.

I didn't use one, as I had handed mine over to Ares and hadn't purchased a new one because they were too expensive…

Ruti was adorably smiling, though, so I didn't take issue with it.

"All right, then, Mogrim, Rit, Ruti, let's get moving."

""""Okay.""""

"Starting tomorrow, we'll be eating preserved rations, but for lunch today I've got fresh lettuce-and-tomato sandwiches."

"""Okay."""

"O-okay?"

"Great. Let's go."

There was a little bit of confusion, but we set off, waking the napping guards at the gate as we ventured beyond Zoltan's limits.

"Take care."

Tisse and Mister Crawly Wawly saw us off, waving as we headed out onto the winter plains.

*   *   *

The dirt-paved Zoltan road swiftly gave way to wild meadow as one marched toward the Wall at the End of the World.

We stayed on course, despite being surrounded by knee-high plants. There was a gentle wind, and the weather was nice. A big cloud hung overhead, a smaller one chasing after it. They almost seemed like a parent and child, which made me chuckle.

"Hmm hmm hmm."

Ruti was humming as she walked. Her big backpack was swaying slightly with her steps, and from time to time it would bounce a little as she hopped over puddles.

"You're in a good mood today, Ruti," I remarked.

Ruti nodded. "This is the first time."

"First time?"

"The first time I've gone on an adventure for you, Big Brother. It's…" She paused for a moment, like she was trying to figure out how best to express it. Ultimately, she gave up and shook her head. "Words can't really begin to describe how great I feel!"

I couldn't help grinning at her excited response. "I'm glad to see you happy," I said.

"Mhmm!" she replied.

I held out my hand, and Ruti grabbed on to it, looking a little bit bashful. The two of us walked like that through the grasses for around three hours.

"Wait."

Rit, who was walking at the head of the group, held out her left hand to stop us. She rested her right on the hilt of one shotel.

"Nrgh, it reeks of goblins!" Mogrim readied his ax.

Ruti had already drawn her goblin blade filled with holes, and I reached for my bronze sword.

"Four to the right and one to the left," Rit said in a quiet voice.

There were five goblins crouching down in the weeds to hide. Likely, they were a band of looters from a tribe that stole money and food from travelers.

The grass swayed as they hurled a volley of spears at us. Rit had already dashed forward, ducking past the projectiles and diving into the grass. In the blink of an eye, she had already cut down two of the goblins. One of the creatures leaped up in surprise and got Mogrim's ax in his head for it. The goblin to the left seemed to be a Sorcerer in the process of casting Fire Arrow.

Just before it could complete its spell, I ran it through with my sword. The magic exploded in a little puff of flame and disappeared. The final goblin had apparently decided that Ruti, with her big back-pack, would be a slow and easy target.

"Ghgi?" called the defeated creature, puzzled.

Ruti never even took a combat stance, merely waving her weapon casually. Just that was enough to split the goblin's armor and body cleanly in two, a feat that caught Mogrim's eye.

"Whoa! That's some cutting edge! What kind of magic blade is that?" he asked excitedly.

No point hurting his dwarven pride by telling him it's just a plain old goblin blade without any kind of magical enhancement...

"That seems to be all of them," I stated.

"Yeah. There don't seem to be any observing from a distance, either," Rit confirmed.

They'd just happened to be lying in wait when we came by. The road on the other side of the city had significantly more traffic, so adventurers would have already taken care of goblins on that side, but the path didn't really see much, so these goblins had gone unnoticed.

"Hmm? What is it, Mogrim?" Glancing around, I noticed he was quietly peering down at the spear that one of our opponents had been wielding. It was a modest weapon, and it looked like it hadn't been properly cared for in a long time.

"It was a long time ago now, but I made this spear."

"...I see..."

Mogrim set the spear down on the ground and murmured a short prayer. The armament's original owner had fallen prey to the goblins.

"Okay, let's walk a little bit more and then have some food. My stomach is telling me it's noon," I said.

"Ha-ha, yeah, that sounds like a plan." Mogrim smiled as he picked up the spear and fastened it to his bag before rejoining us, taking the lead.

This world was filled with combat. But even so, it would be miserable to go through existence always just mourning and suffering.

Even after a fight, we could sit down to laugh and enjoy fresh, colorful sandwiches for lunch. Time spent together with trusty friends was the same no matter how the world was.

*   *   *

"This is where Gideon is," Yarandrala muttered as she looked up at the sign for the apothecary.

A mix of anticipation and unease crossed her face, and there was a breathtaking beauty in the tinge of anxiety in her gaze. However, it was the sort of allure that gave her a distant air.

"Well, they're out now, though." Godwin pointed half-heartedly at the CLOSED sign on the door, as if he was already tired of seeing that blend of emotions on Yarandrala's face. "There's no sign of them inside, either. Maybe they decided to take the day off and go on a date somewhere."

Yarandrala glared at Godwin for a split second before softly pressing a finger to the door. With her abilities, it would be simple to force it open, but she recoiled after a beat.

"So then, what sort of place would the two of them go?"

"How should I know?"

"Then where is the nearest guard outpost?"

"W-wait. Just hold on a minute. I'm thinking," Godwin pleaded. It wasn't as though he were especially close with Red or Rit. However, if he admitted as much to Yarandrala now, she'd have no further use for him.

If I did that, she really would turn me over to the guards.

Yarandrala seemed to be Red's acquaintance. That Godwin had claimed to be Red's friend was probably why she had not brought him in despite realizing he was a criminal. His safe escape from Zoltan hinged upon reuniting Yarandrala and Red.

"For now, how about we try checking where Rit lived before she moved in here?" Godwin suggested.

"Very well. Lead the way."

Godwin started toward Rit's old abode downtown.

I can't imagine the two of them being there, but I only need to stall for a bit of time until they return to the shop.

With that in mind, Godwin chose a slightly indirect route, a decision that ultimately proved unfortunate.

As they were walking along, a voice called from the other side of the street.

"Yarandrala!"

"Ghk." A cold sweat formed on Godwin's back. The merchant who had been traveling to Zoltan with the high elf was running toward her.

"Yarandrala! That guy's face and voice are different, but I'm sure that's Godwin! I checked with local law enforcement, and Godwin apparently escaped from prison and went missing."

"Th— Surely this is just a case of mistaken identity." Godwin flashed an ingratiating smile, trying to look for all the world like an average, harmless person, but the merchant jabbed his finger at the disguised man.

"That shit-eating grin is one hundred percent Godwin! Way back, he worked at my shop as a trainee and stole the money out of my shop! I had to close because of him! And he had that exact same expression then, too!"

Godwin was growing more nervous by the second.

During his tenure under the merchant's employ, Godwin had been a low-level nobody in the Thieves Guild, which meant doing those sorts of petty robberies. Godwin didn't consider the idea of fated retribution often, but that sure seemed like what this was.

While Godwin's face tensed as he raced to conjure up an excuse, Yarandrala glared at him scornfully before sighing and turning to face the merchant.

"This man is apparently a friend of Rit the hero and Red, so perhaps it really is just a case of mistaken identity?"

"Preposterous! He sent a bunch of demons after Rit and kidnapped a boy named Al whom she was protecting! This man's the worst kind of criminal! There's no way such a despicable ruffian would be friends with her!"

All of a sudden, the air around the group changed. There was a murderous intent unlike anything the people who lived in Zoltan had ever felt. Yarandrala's clenched teeth ground audibly, and she was gripping her quarterstaff so tightly that her knuckles turned pale.

Oh shit! Something in there hit a nerve!

On instinct alone, Godwin understood that this furious woman was as powerful as Rit the hero, if not more so. The yellow mask covering Godwin's face slipped to the ground.

"You betrayed her trust, too?"

"N-no! This is a misunderstanding! W-we were on opposite sides then, but there was a reconciliation after some other things happened!"

The paved road warped, swelling up before shattering. Vegetation that would have taken centuries to break through suddenly erupted in a single instant. An enormous green monster formed before Yarandrala. At the center of the mass of wriggling vines was a large red flower.

"An elderflower great spirit?!"

Panic gripped the hapless Godwin. This was a special kind of spirit beast that even a relatively high-level Alchemist like him had never seen before.

"I'm going to take them with me. I won't let anyone wrong them again."

Vines covered in vicious thorns rose into the air to pummel Godwin into the ground. A single blow would be enough to kill him.

Godwin had no idea why Yarandrala had gotten so enraged, but he could tell this wasn't something he could weasel his way out of. The man glanced around, looking for any kind of help, but unsurprisingly, the merchant who had exposed him and the others nearby paid him no heed as they fled.

Not sure what I expected.

He was a criminal, a real villain. His fellows had vanished after Bighawk's fall. There was no way anyone would stand up to a fearsome flower monster to help someone like him.

I always knew this was the kind of end waiting for me, but now that it's time...I realize that being all alone sucks...

Gripped by fear though he was, Godwin still attempted to stagger away, if only to prolong his life a few extra moments.

Suddenly, there was a whinny, and Godwin felt something invisible tug at his body. Just when he was on the verge of collapsing, a saddled horse with a chestnut coat galloped up beside him. Godwin reflexively clung to the animal, and the moment he did, it charged past the green monster. The vines came crashing down, but the horse evaded the attacks gracefully, like it was being directed by a skilled rider.

"What the hell?"

There was no one riding the horse.

"Ah!" But then Godwin noticed the tiny figure on the horse's head. "You're that spider!"

Mister Crawly Wawly was unhurriedly moving all eight of his legs up and down. He was the one directing the horse. He glanced back at Godwin and raised one of his front legs in greeting.

"Wh-why did you save me?"

Godwin struggled to comprehend what exactly was transpiring. Yet no matter how he looked at it, the reality of the situation was right there in front of him.

This little spider rescued me.

He considered the possibility that the arachnid was here on Tisse's orders, but if that was the case, it would have been surer for the girl to come herself. And it wasn't like Tisse had any reason to risk herself for Godwin.

"Hey, spider, why did you save me?"

Godwin expected no response, of course, but Mister Crawly Wawly, still facing forward, just tilted his head in evident confusion. Then he began gesturing confidently with his forelegs. The message was plain, even without actual words.

"We're friends because we fought together...and it's only natural to help a friend in need."

Godwin was a criminal who had worked with the Thieves Guild, but that meant nothing to Mister Crawly Wawly. Complicated things like that were of no concern to him.

"You..."

Godwin had survived on the whim of a tiny spider. Even so, the man felt something warm inside himself as he watched the arachnid direct the horse.

"Sorry. And thank you."

Obviously, spiders had no expressions. Yet when Godwin saw Mister Crawly Wawly glance back at him, it felt like the creature was smiling.

It's been a long time since I've felt such sincere gratitude.

Without his realizing it, a gentle grin had crossed Godwin's lips.

Unfortunately, just as the bud of friendship was sprouting between the little spider and the villainous Alchemist, the verdant monster thrust its vines into the ground. Yarandrala touched its flower and closed her eyes as she wove a spell.

"Child of mana dwelling beneath the earth, heed my call and arise. Thorn Bind!"

Following her songlike chant, a swell of magic power ran through the earth. The road in front of the horse cracked, and several brambles sprang forth, ready to snare.

"Give me a little thread!" Godwin shouted.

Taking the spider silk from Mister Crawly Wawly, he mixed it together in his hand with some hairs from the horse's mane, a handful of dirt, and several drops of his own blood.

"Skill: Instant Alchemy! Advanced Alchemy: Constricting Net!"

Godwin hurled the paste-like substance he'd created. It expanded in the air to become a net that covered the thorny hedges standing in their path. And the next moment, it constricted violently, compressing the vines into a single bundle.

"Now!"

Mister Crawly Wawly's legs danced and, seeming to understand, the horse dashed through the gap Godwin's net had created.

"Hoooo! That's something. Is this horse a friend of yours, too?"

Mister Crawly Wawly swayed in response, and the horse whinnied as if to agree.

Godwin laughed at himself for having asked so absurd a thing. He couldn't help feeling like he wanted to be friends with the two of them, however.

I'm really starting to lose it now, aren't I?

Godwin grimaced, but quickly reverted to a pleasant sort of smile that didn't really suit him. He started to believe that he would escape. Yarandrala was far behind now, and her plant beast was quite slow. Mister Crawly Wawly's horse friend was so powerful and swift that Godwin could only wonder where this fine steed had been hiding in Zoltan.

If they could clear the plaza downtown, they would reach an area with more people, hopefully keeping the high elf from using such flashy abilities.

Godwin's hopes were quickly dashed, though, when he turned and spied Yarandrala grabbing the conjured vines and getting into some kind of stance.

She murmured something.

"Release."

And then she went flying.

"Th-the hell?! She used that great spirit like a catapult!"

The high elf arced through the air and was back on the horse's heels in moments.

"O great monarch of the forests of old! Ruler of mana, origin of all!"

Fractures ran all through the plaza where the upper crust of Zoltan society went about their leisure. The ten or so people in the area ran in terror as they saw a figure rise from beneath the ground.

"Wh-what are you doing summoning something that huge here?!" Godwin screamed.

Yarandrala did not appear to pay him any heed, and a great tree spirit destroyed the plaza as it slowly rose from the ground.

On closer inspection, tendrils were grasping those too slow to escape and carefully carrying them to safety. Thankfully, Yarandrala was at least ensuring her actions didn't injure innocent bystanders. Godwin still had to believe there was a way for someone so powerful to fight without so much property damage.

It was baffling that a hero could engage in these decidedly unheroic actions, but when Godwin glimpsed Yarandrala's face, he realized what was going on.

"She's so mad that she snapped?"

He felt a chill run down his spine. A valiant soul like her had been so enraged by a two-bit lowlife like him that she had lost herself in anger. What had he done to provoke that?

Yarandrala had summoned a terrifying spirit in the middle of town. Godwin had never seen that manner of entity in person before, but he

understood enough to know it could destroy all of Zoltan if Yarandrala wished it.

"Run!"

There was no way to fight that. The Alchemist, spider, and horse
continued to flee, but an enormous tendril as thick as the road was
wide swung down at them.

"Uoohhh?!"

Even the incredible horse could not fully evade in time and was knocked
aside, throwing Godwin and Mister Crawly Wawly to the ground.

"Argh. Are you okay?"

"Neeeeigh…"

Staggering to his feet, Godwin saw that one of the horse's legs had
been injured. It wouldn't be able to run with that. All Godwin could
do now was make a break for it on his own two legs, so he started looking for Mister Crawly Wawly.

"Wh-what are you doing?"

The little spider was staring down the enormous tree spirit that tow-
ered above the plaza and waving his front legs to block its path.

Why? Even Godwin understood the answer this time. Mister Crawly
Wawly had a friend who needed protecting.

The spider turned to Godwin.

"I…I…" Godwin subconsciously edged backward, feeling pathetic
as his legs buckled.

Mister Crawly Wawly gestured with his front legs. Seeing that, the
fallen horse whinnied softly.

"Y-you're telling me to run away?"

It looked like the horse and spider were both nodding.

Godwin felt something curious welling up within himself. He
slammed his fist into his trembling legs and hurriedly gathered several
things scattered around on the ground.

"Fragments of glass, mud, insect wings… I can make the missing
water using my blood and some dirt… Instant Alchemy! Intermediate
Alchemy: Vulcanized Crystallization!"

Godwin flicked his wrist as a liquid formed in the palm of his hand. The substance hardened in midair, forming into a thin, serrated, swordlike crystal—an instant alchemical weapon. Godwin held the blade in his right hand and stood next to Mister Crawly Wawly.

"Don't worry, horse. I'm a master Alchemist, so I'll make you some medicine that can fix that leg in no time."

What was there to gain from helping a horse or spider? They weren't rich, nor were they beautiful women. Godwin hadn't been ordered by some bigwig to safeguard them.

"This is kinda refreshing."

A grin crossed Godwin's face as he readied his makeshift blade. Mister Crawly Wawly gleefully hopped onto his shoulder.

"All right, do your worst, you damn monster! I'm the greatest Alchemist in Zoltan!"

The great spirit raised its green limbs and swung them down at Godwin and Mister Crawly Wawly.

"Uoooooooohhhhhhhhhhhhhhh!!!" Godwin roared as he swung his weapon...

"No matter how you look at it, you have no chance of winning, so please just run away." A little shadow appeared in front of the tendrils that were hurtling down at them. "I admit you've gone up a bit in my book, though."

The deadly vines were cut to pieces.

"Tisse!"

There was a hint of kindness in the girl's eyes as she glanced at Godwin and the spider riding on his shoulder. She tossed him a bag with her free hand. Catching it, Godwin quickly realized what it was from the feel alone.

"An alchemy set! Thanks!"

"Please use that to escape with the horse."

"But what about you?!"

Tisse raised her left hand in place of an answer. Mister Crawly Wawly leaped from Godwin's shoulder to her hand.

"I have no idea what is happening, but if someone is running wild

in Zoltan, then as a Zoltan adventurer, I have a responsibility to stop them."

"Oh, hey! Where's Ms. Ruhr? And Rit and Red?"

"They're all out of town right now. I'm the only one still here."

Tisse jumped to evade the tendril bearing down on her. A dozen more vines swarmed her in the air, but Tisse just held out her left palm and then changed trajectories as though something were tugging on her.

"This is nice. Lots of tall obstacles all around and plenty of places to hide. Perfect for me to really fight properly."

Tisse was controlling Mister Crawly Wawly's thread using her left hand. By sticking the spider silk to a nearby building, she could freely move even while off the ground.

Tisse and Mister Crawly Wawly dodged the great spirit's attacks and cut down its tendrils one after the other as they drew closer to Yarandrala. Godwin, meanwhile, had the wounded horse drink the medicine he'd made with the alchemy set as he beheld the battle.

"Dammit. What do I do...?"

If he could just get Yarandrala to calm down a bit, they could explain that Tisse and Red were close friends. But Godwin had no clue how to go about that.

"Wait just a minute, please, Yarandrala! Please listen! The person you're fighting right now is Tisse! She's Red's friend!"

Unfortunately, Godwin's shouts fell on deaf ears as Yarandrala continued to fight using the great tree spirit. Tisse and Mister Crawly Wawly kept flirting with disaster, just barely avoiding the vines coming from all directions as Godwin desperately tried to think of something to do.

Despair gripped Godwin as the newfound bravery in his heart began to wither. And that was when he heard a familiar voice.

"Well, this is a right old mess."

Turning around, Godwin saw an old lady with a walking stick sighing as she watched the skirmish between Tisse and Yarandrala.

"M-Master Mistorm?!"

"Oh, if it isn't Godwin. Still getting up to mischief? Didn't I tell you to cut that out and be a good boy?"

"This isn't the time for that! Please do something to stop them!"

Master Mistorm put her hand to her chin as she peered down at Godwin. "Tell me everything you know."

*　　　　*　　　　*

Humans! Damn humans!

High elves did not get angry without reason, but their fury was like a raging fire when they were provoked. They valued trust above all else, viewing disloyalty as the worst sin.

To Yarandrala, that Gideon had disappeared was incomprehensible. His comrades giving up on him without trying to search for the man was not only harder to believe but also absolutely unforgivable. That was why she had abandoned the quest to save the world. To her, the party's betrayal of Gideon weighed more heavily than the fate of the world.

After she left the group, Yarandrala had gone to the Duchy of Loggervia, thinking that Gideon would go to Rit if he was feeling hurt. However, he hadn't been there, and neither had Rit.

Rit had fought and bled for her country and had given her all for the restoration of her homeland, even though it meant leaving Gideon's side. That same woman who had done so much for Loggervia had left because she had become an obstacle to the crown prince's succession to the throne.

It wounded Yarandrala as surely as any knife. Two whom she dearly loved had been betrayed by the very people they had protected. They had gone unrewarded and abandoned for their troubles.

After that, Yarandrala continued on her own, tracking Rit. Whenever she heard rumors of Rit's travels, her heart felt like it would split in two. Yet when she heard from Godwin that there was someone at her side, someone who might be Gideon, she had been elated. The thought of finally meeting the two of them again had been the final hope supporting her troubled heart.

But they had not been here. What's more, the human who had claimed to be their friend turned out to be an enemy who had betrayed their trust.

Why do Gideon and Rit have to suffer such a fate? Why must every human seek to hurt them?

Godwin's desperate pleas would never suffice. Yarandrala would crush her beloved friends' enemies and then take them back with her to the high elf country of Kiramin so that they would never have to suffer such mistreatment again.

Yarandrala was driven by a mix of love and savage rage as she continued to fight.

"Smash her down!"

Innumerable tendrils swarmed Tisse, but she continued to evade them using Mister Crawly Wawly's thread and her exquisite swordsmanship. Tisse moved in close to Yarandrala several times, but the high elf was skilled with her quarterstaff, and she did not allow Tisse to land a blow.

The battle seemed to be at something of a stalemate.

"O polar winds, O life-stealing chill! Blizzard!"

Suddenly, a violent chill enveloped the tree spirit, sealing its body in ice.

Yarandrala's furious gaze shot to the source of the magic. "Who are you?" she demanded.

Standing there was an old lady wielding a staff.

"You really did a number on our town," the elderly woman remarked.

"You're—!" Tisse shouted.

"Tisse. I had no idea you were so skilled."

"And I never would have guessed you could use such powerful magic, Mistorm."

"Ah-ha-ha-ha. I'm glad we could get to know each other better. So have you cooled your head a little bit, high elf missy?"

"I don't want to be called 'missy' by someone who hasn't even lived half as long as I have," Yarandrala shot back.

The ice sealing the great spirit began to crack as its body trembled.

"Personally, I'd kind of like being called that no matter how many years I've got under my belt... Looks like my magic isn't enough to stop you, though!"

"However, with the two of us fighting together, it would be quite difficult for you, right?"

Even with Tisse's words, Yarandrala did not show any sign of backing down.

"Yarandrala! Listen up! We're friends of Red and Rit!" Mistorm called out.

"The trifling words of a human can't be trusted!" Yarandrala shouted back. She remained unmoved. However, Tisse was stunned to hear the high elf's name.

Yarandrala?! The one who was Ruti's comrade?!

It certainly explained why she was so strong.

"In that case, just ask them yourself!" insisted Mistorm.

Yarandrala frowned at that. "Where are they?!"

"Ah, I can answer that one," Tisse chimed in.

"Who are you?" demanded the indignant high elf.

"Uh, umm...I'm a friend of theirs."

Tisse decided to hide the fact that she had been a member of the Hero's party herself. Like Ruti's, her face was largely expressionless and difficult to read, but she understood the feelings of others better.

She had been added to the Hero's party as Red's—Gideon's—replacement. Mentioning that to Yarandrala would only stoke the flames, however.

"So then, where are they?" Yarandrala asked again, fixing Tisse with a piercing gaze.

"They should be on their way to the Wall at the End of the World."

"What? There's no passage through the mountains to the east from here."

"You're right. Red, who I suspect is indeed the person you think him to be, is going there to get a gemstone for a ring to give Rit," Tisse explained, observing Yarandrala's expression as she chose her words carefully.

How will the high elf react?

"Gideon? A ring for Rit?"

Tisse panicked a little when Yarandrala used Red's real name, but fortunately, the high elf's voice was little more than a whisper, so only Tisse's sharp ears caught it.

"Really?"

"Yes."

The crack in the ice holding the great spirit suddenly widened. Once free, the monstrous thing roared before disappearing in a cloud of flowers and white mana. Petals swirled around Yarandrala, gradually lowering her to the ground. With her adversary finally quelled, Tisse landed, too. The high elf was still plainly wary, but at least she wasn't attacking anyone.

"Phew."

Tisse wiped the sweat from her brow as she sheathed her sword. Mister Crawly Wawly shifted to her pocket, tired from everything that had happened, and curled up to rest.

""""Hoorayyyyy!!!""""" came cheers from all sides.

To Tisse's astonishment, people who had been hiding just outside the plaza gathered around her.

"Thank you so much! That was a magnificent battle!"

"I was worried about what to do when Rit the Hero retired and Albert and Bui left, but it's a relief to know someone like you is in town!"

"Please allow me to treat you to dinner at my mansion sometime!"

"Do you mind if I sell steamed buns with your face on them at my store?"

"You were flying around like an angel, miss!"

Yarandrala, the cause of the rampage, was still alive and well, but the laid-back Zoltanis could not help showering Tisse with praise for the heroic spectacle she had given them.

Although internally baffled by the praise, Tisse remained expressionless. This was something an Assassin should ordinarily not be on the receiving end of. She was exceedingly embarrassed.

"Still, you really made a showy mess of things here," Mistorm stated with exasperation as Yarandrala stood there dumbfounded.

The great spirit had disappeared, but the plaza was a scene of utter destruction. The ground was torn up, and the surrounding buildings were off-kilter, tilted down to their foundations. Massive reconstruction was going to be needed.

"...My apologies."

Yarandrala still did not trust these humans, but she did at least recognize her own misdeeds.

"Well, what's done is done. Fortunately, no one seems to have been hurt. You took care not to injure any bystanders, right?" Mistorm said with a smile.

However, given the destruction, Tisse suspected that not all of the residents would be able to just laugh it off. And sure enough, a well-dressed, mustachioed middle-aged man approached Yarandrala.

"You, high elf. I don't know what all happened, but I'd like an explanation. Who gave you the right to wreak havoc on our town like that?"

Yarandrala glanced over at Godwin. The man had been trying to sneak away while hiding his face from the crowd. And seeing the horse walking in front of Godwin to help conceal him, Yarandrala smiled ever so slightly. Then she turned to the well-dressed man who had approached her.

"I was searching for someone. I thought that the person who was guiding me to them had deceived me because of a misunderstanding, and I got angry."

"Huh? That's it?"

"Yes, that's it."

"Preposterous! Causing such an enormous incident over something like that is..." The man surveyed the destruction around him before facing Yarandrala again, looking at her like he would at a monster.

Yarandrala pulled out a small bag and handed it to the man.

"My personal circumstances have nothing to do with you all, so I apologize for the trouble. I understand that regardless of my apology, what I've done is not something that can readily be forgiven, but I would at least like to provide adequate recompense."

"Hmph. Payment with such a tiny bag? Even if they're gold coins, there can't be more than ten in— What?!"

The man's formal tone cracked as he was overcome by shock. Curious about what had happened, others gathered around to look, but upon seeing the shine from inside the satchel, they just shook their heads in confusion.

"What's the baron gawking at? It's just a few silvers."

"But aren't payrils a different size? And the color's a little different, too."

"F-fools! These are elven coins! A single one is worth ten thousand payrils!"

"T-ten thousand?! Ummm, how many silvers is ten thousand payrils anyway...?"

"Ten thousand, you dolt! And there are seven elven coins here! Seventy thousand payrils is enough to rebuild the assembly from the ground up with plenty to spare!"

"What?!"

"That's crazy! Are you really giving us that much?!"

When Yarandrala nodded, the residents started whooping and hollering around the ruined plaza about how they were going to throw a huge party with all that money.

There did not seem to be anyone still angry at the high elf. She'd been ready to flee if they tried to arrest her. Thus, her sudden absolution was perplexing.

"What a hopeless bunch," Mistorm commented with a chuckle as she watched people celebrate by tossing both the middle-aged baron and Tisse into the air. "That's just how folk here act, I suppose. No point worrying about the past."

"But the plaza is still destroyed," Yarandrala reminded her.

"That's hardly uncommon! Zoltan's hit by storms all the time. Every year, some buildings get toppled and crops get wrecked. It can be a right old mess. But the weather doesn't care what those on the ground think, right? If something gets destroyed, just build it again. It's better to smile than be sad. You're only missing out if you don't. That's the Zoltan way of thinking, at least."

Yarandrala's brow furrowed slightly. "Are you calling me a storm?"

"In a sense. I trust if you genuinely went all out, there'd be no stopping you. Getting angry at you would be like shaking one's fist at a hurricane."

"…" Yarandrala silently watched the people cheering.

Sensing that the high elf's ire had settled completely, Mistorm breathed a sigh of relief.

While still being flung in the air, Tisse called out to the two women. "It's all well and good for you to continue chatting, but do you think you could help me out now?"

"Oops." Seeing that Tisse was at a complete loss over what to do with the sudden adulation, Mistorm headed over to the crowd with a smile on her face.

✳   ✳   ✳

"All right."

Tisse, Mister Crawly Wawly, Yarandrala, Mistorm, and Godwin headed to a small restaurant after leaving the plaza.

"I thought we should have a little something to eat. This place is a favorite of mine," Mistorm said as she started in on the large plate of pasta with a meaty red sauce that had been set in front of her.

"That's beside the point. I need to find Gid—"

"Red, right?" Tisse hurriedly cut Yarandrala off.

The high elf glared at her, but Tisse just eyed the woman back.

"You said that Red and Rit are heading for the Wall at the End of the World, right?" Yarandrala asked.

"Yes," Tisse confirmed.

"So that Red can make a ring to give to Rit?"

"Yes."

"Huh, he always seems like such a wuss, but I guess he does have some stones after all," Godwin quipped, eliciting a scowl from Yarandrala that forced him to look away hurriedly.

"...Thank goodness..."

Tisse did not miss the high elf's whisper. She had never interacted with Yarandrala before. By the time she had met Ruti and the others, Yarandrala had already left the party. There had been plenty of stories, but now that Tisse had interacted with Yarandrala firsthand, the high elf made quite a different impression from what Tisse had first imagined.

"That hits the spot."

Mistorm had cleared half the big plate of pasta in the blink of an eye. None of the other three had so much as touched their orders. Mister Crawly Wawly did seem to be enjoying a fly he had caught after the scent of the pasta had drawn it.

"We're going to chase after Red and Rit, yes? It's going to be far more than a day trip, so you should eat now while you can," Mistorm chided.

"'We'?" Yarandrala asked suspiciously.

"If you want to find those two, Tisse will have to guide you. It just so happens that I have business with Mogrim, who's traveling with Red and Rit, and Godwin here is just along for the ride."

"Huh? Me too?"

"Yep, you're coming with, kiddo."

"Why should I?"

"Now, now, don't complain. I've got my reasons, so be a good boy and just do as I say."

"'Be a good boy'... You know I was pretty high up in the Thieves

Guild, right? I've never been able to deal with you, though," the Alchemist admitted.

Tisse was surprised to see Godwin accept Mistorm's instructions so readily. She turned to the old woman and asked, "I don't mind guiding Yarandrala, but what business do you have with Mogrim?"

"Mink, Mogrim's wife, said he was probably headed to the Wall and asked me to lend him a hand."

"Ahh. Yes, he went with Red and Rit to try to get his hands on some earth crystal," Tisse explained.

"I didn't expect that. I was sure Mogrim would assemble a group of adventurers, but I would never have guessed he'd go with Rit and Red. I had planned to catch him at the Adventurers Guild, but by the time Mink told me what her husband was planning, he'd already left town. I was preparing to depart right when that mess in the plaza got underway."

"Sorry about that," Yarandrala apologized.

"It worked out in its own way. We've got a nice little group of companions for the journey," Mistorm said before turning back to her plate.

"Do we really need to make such an effort? They only left early this morning, and it's noon now. If we chase after them on horses or riding drakes, we should catch up by tomorrow evening," Tisse remarked.

"A journey's a journey, no matter the length," Mistorm responded with a smile.

"Indeed." Yarandrala nodded before turning to the pasta in front of her with elegant poise.

"So long as I don't end up hanging from the gallows, that's enough for me. And if I'm going to end up dying anyway, I'd rather it be after I eat some delicious food," Godwin declared as he dove into his meal with gusto.

"Are you not going to eat?" Mistorm asked Tisse.

"I will."

The young Assassin was worried about Ruti, Red's true identity, and several other things, but she decided to let those be and trust Red to figure something out as she turned her attention to the pasta in front of her.

"Delicious."

"Right?"

The flavor certainly merited Tisse's attention. She made a quick mental note of the restaurant's name.

Chapter 3

The Mushroom Forest Zoogs

We received a warm welcome at the zoog village when we arrived at dusk the day after setting out. The plan was to ask the zoogs for directions to the gem giant village. This settlement was in the middle of the forest, where the canopy of foliage blotted out the sun's light.

We were sitting on large mushrooms, across a moss-covered fallen tree from the zoog elder.

"It'sh been a while," the elder greeted me in a friendly tone, shaking my hand as the tentacles around its mouth quivered.

Zoogs were a slightly grotesque sort of monster. They were large, cat-size rodents with beard-like tentacles around their mouths. Their hands and feet were more similar to those of monkeys than those of rodents, and they were dexterous enough to handle tools.

The zoog warriors standing behind the elder wielded spears with stone tips and wore armor woven from layers of bark.

"I know it'sh a long way from Zoltan, but it would be nishe if you shtopped by every onshe in a while like you ushed to."

"I'm sorry for being away for so long. I found myself a partner and have had trouble finding the time to get away from Zoltan."

"Truly? That'sh wonderful. I've heard that humansh have difficulty pairing off."

The elder drew close to my finger, gently wrapping a tentacle around it. Mogrim tensed up, but I flashed a reassuring smile.

"Thank you very much. May our friendship continue to be blessed."

"May it be blesshed indeed."

Zoogs considered the tentacles around their mouths crucial organs, and if one was injured, the zoog would become incredibly ill for quite a long time. Allowing something so essential to be touched by another was a sign of utmost trust for a zoog. Their tentacles had a spongy sort of texture that felt nice when you got used to it.

"I've brought a gift both as an apology for not visiting for so long and also because there was something I was hoping I could ask your help with."

I laid out the pork. It was about a whole hog's worth of meat.

"Ooooh. We are grateful for your generoshity."

The warriors standing behind the elder started to whisper excitedly when they saw the large slabs of meat.

"We can never get enough meat. It would be nishe if we could undershtand commershe." The elder scratched its furry neck a bit. "But if wishesh were fishesh. We are jusht grateful to have friendsh willing to share with ush like thish. Shomeone, pleashe take the meat to the preparation tree."

"Feel free to take most of it. A little is plenty for my companions and me. We would like to have some mushrooms and fruits as well," I said.

"Heh-heh! In that cashe we'll be glad to accommodate you."

Hearing that, the zoogs around us looked at each other and smiled excitedly.

✳   ✳   ✳

"You really have a mysterious bunch of connections, Red."

Rit seemed to be enjoying taking in the sights as we strolled through the zoog village.

Zoogs were monsters, but they had developed a civilization of sorts.

To our left were branches lined up with lots and lots of mushrooms growing from them—a farming plot. To our right were zoogs kneading clay.

"That's how they make earthenware. They don't have kilns, so they just roast it on a fire, but there's a uniqueness to the hand-drawn patterns that's quite lovely," I explained.

A young zoog working on one piece noticed us and stopped to peer nervously. Rit waved her hand a little, and the young zoog emphatically waved both its hands, black from the dirt, back and forth.

"Ah-ha-ha-ha. I've never met a zoog before, but I would never have expected them to take so kindly to people," admitted Rit.

"Ordinarily, they probably wouldn't," I said.

"Really?"

I nodded. "Zoogs have boundless curiosity. They are more willing to risk interacting because the oddity of a seemingly friendly human they've never met captures their interest. However, if they encounter a human they don't know in the forest, they're just as liable to kill them."

"So on that point, they definitely are monsters." Despite Rit's clear enjoyment, Mogrim's face was tense, and his hand hovered over his ax. "Are we really going to spend the night in a den of man-eating monsters?"

"They don't attack people they are on good terms with, and zoogs aren't particularly strong, either. Don't tell me the valiant drake slayer is actually scared of a bunch of little zoogs?" I teased.

"Bite your tongue! Of course I'm not scared!" Mogrim glared at me overly defensively. The menacing look was enough to send the zoogs watching from a distance diving for cover.

"See? You scared them," I observed.

"Mrgh… Still, is this really going to be okay? Are they going to think I'm an enemy now and sneak up on me while I'm sleeping?"

"Not a chance. I presented them a gift when we arrived, and they accepted it. Despite how they may look, zoogs take promises extremely seriously."

"What?"

"On that point, they are a bit of a good fit for dwarves," I stated.

"Hmm. Keeping your word is certainly a virtue."

Promises were important to dwarves. Dwarves highly valued oaths sworn under mutual consent. Even if it was one made with someone they hated or they knew that keeping their word would put them at a disadvantage, they believed in doing their utmost to uphold their end of a promise.

And learning that zoogs had that point in common with them, Mogrim eased up a bit on his wariness.

"That's mighty respectable for a bunch of monsters."

Mogrim joined Rit in having fun looking around at the creatures going about their lives.

"When you think about it, the dim light beneath the trees and the damp air is reminiscent of dwarven caverns," Mogrim remarked.

"You came out to Zoltan from Sir Beard Mountain, didn't you?" I asked.

"Indeed. The missus went out that way as a traveling merchant, and it was love at first sight. I'd like to show her around there someday, but given my situation, I can't ever return."

"For a group that puts such a heavy weight on keeping promises, that's a pretty hot-blooded sort of reaction," I said.

"Mhm. Because we live our lives following the rules, if we ever do happen to run into something that pushes us to betray those values, we can end up acting impulsively," Mogrim replied.

Dwarves were indeed fastidious when it came to rules, which was why I was always a bit surprised that Mogrim had run off with Mink, but I guess it was precisely because dwarves were so strict that he had. Maybe that was also why romance stories written by humans were secretly so popular among dwarves.

Looking up, Mogrim suddenly let out a shout. Two zoog children were hanging from a branch overhead. Seeing them, Ruti and I immediately started running. There was a snapping sound as the tree limb broke. The zoogs' scream resounded.

"Ruti!"

"I know!"

My sister moved in front of me and interlaced her fingers, and I leaped up onto her hands.

"Yah!"

Ruti poured strength into her arms and sent me flying. Her aim was true, and I caught the two zoogs falling through the air.

"Rit!"

"On it! Levitate!"

My body started floating before slowly descending to the ground. Rit's levitation magic could only target one person. With two zoogs plummeting at the same time, she would only have been able to save one, but if I caught the two of them, and then Rit ensorcelled me, we would all three be able to land safely.

"Are you okay?" Touching down, I gently checked on the two zoogs clinging to me.

The kitten-size creatures' black, pearl-like eyes spun as they tried to understand what had happened. When they finally processed everything, tears welled up in their eyes, and they clung to me and started bawling.

"Um…uh…"

I was at a loss. I had no clue how to soothe zoog children. I glanced at the others, looking for some kind of help, but they just had a kindly look in their eyes, like they were watching some heartwarming scene. I couldn't deny that it was, but I also had no idea what to do with the children hanging on me. Perhaps I would've understood had I been a father.

I should get Mogrim to handle this as practice, since he's about to become a father himself! I thought.

"Cuckoo! Nahko! I'm sho glad you're shafe!"

""Mommy!""

The two zoogs clinging to me jumped into their mother's embrace.

"Phew." Relieved everything had turned out all right, I wiped away the tears and drool left on my clothes.

*   *   *

That night, we enjoyed an enormous feast.

"Shu shu! Eat and drink ash much ash you like."

In the banquet hall, the zoogs were drinking alcohol made from tree sap while singing and dancing merrily. The moss covering the trees of the forest was illuminating the surroundings with a tranquil light. Some type of luminescent strain, I supposed.

"Thank you sho much for shaving our children."

"How can we ever repay you?"

The kids we had rescued were apparently pretty closely related to a zoog leader and thus fairly high status. Zoogs had a parliamentary system of leadership. They didn't have a firm culture of individual ownership, so rank for them was different from the human idea of it. It wasn't an exact fit, but to put things simply, the children were akin to nobility.

In zoog society, the farther up you lived on a tree, the greater your social standing, from living down at the roots to living in the tree's trunk, out on the limbs, and on the leaves. You would think that might lead to a lot of incidents like today's, but the timbers they made their homes in were stout and resilient. A limb snapping without any warning was almost unheard of.

Anyway, because the kids we helped turned out to be high status, our reception at the banquet was top class.

"You were amazing! Wash that magic?" one zoog inquired.

"That wasn't magic. It was the bond Big Brother and I share—our sibling power," Ruti answered.

"Really?! I love my big brother, too! Do you think I can be like you shomeday, Missh Ruti?!"

"So you're a sister as well? Yes, if you always stay together and get along with each other, I'm sure you can."

"Yay!"

Ruti seemed to be getting along well with the children we had saved. She had experienced so many adventures as the Hero, but it felt like it had been a long time since I had seen her just mingling and enjoying herself with something unrelated to combat. Back at the start of the journey, when her blessing was still weak, there had been moments like this. Around the time we left the capital, she had reached a point where things didn't affect her anymore.

I was delighted to see Ruti appreciating interacting with others, even if it was just at a little village two days' walk from Zoltan.

"Good."

A bowl of mushroom soup was placed in front of me. Turning around, I saw Rit smiling kindly.

"I'm sure Ruti liked traveling with you before, but I don't think she's ever enjoyed the journey itself," she said.

"Yeah. But now she can smile... I'm so happy for her."

Rit leaned her shoulder against mine.

The cooking had a bit of spicy seasoning, but it was delicious. And zoog spirits went well with hot food. Drumbeats and the trills of a wooden flute made from a hollowed tree branch intermingled as pairs of zoogs danced odd steps.

"You runts aren't half-bad!"

Mogrim's face was red from all the booze as he strutted, too, determined not to lose to the zoogs. The short, stout dwarf held hands with a zoog and joined in the revelry.

The zoogs seemed shocked at the sudden intrusion, but before long, their curiosity about the unknown got the best of them, and Mogrim was bombarded with dance requests.

Even a tough dwarf like him finally had to beg off, though, collapsing with a satisfied grin. At that, the zoogs smiled and clapped.

"Red." Rit grabbed my arm. Her cheeks were flushed from drink, which just made her all the more beautiful. "Why didn't you ever introduce me to such a fun group?"

"I'm sorry. We can come back another time just for fun, if you want," I responded.

"Yeah! Ooh, this is a good one. Say ahhh."

"H-hey...not in front of other people... Fine, fine... Ahhh."

The roasted mushroom Rit put in my mouth was simple, just a little bit of salt for seasoning, but it was fresh and delicious nonetheless.

*   *   *

We spent the night in the zoog village. Come morning, we began our climb up the mountains. Our goal was a cave the zoogs had told us of.

"Ohh, the snow's piled up." Mogrim was getting excited as he stepped onto the thin layer of frost that had built up in the shade of the trees. The air was clear, and Zoltan was visible in the distance.

"It's a wonderful view," Rit commented. Her ears had gotten red, so I covered them with my hands, which earned me a tickled laugh.

"It's a good thing the gem giants aren't near the summit," I said.

"Yeah. The three of us can endure extreme cold, and I'm sure a dwarf like Mogrim can deal with the mountain climate, but cold is still cold," Rit responded.

"Part of the reason I came to Zoltan was because I wanted a warmer climate...which is how I ended up with you, so I prefer hot summers."

"Weren't you complaining about the heat during the summer?"

"Ah-ha-ha, I forgot about that."

A fox peeked out from the trees, peering intently at the odd sight of a dwarf and humans. A lump of snow was knocked from a branch by a sudden gust of wind and fell on the beast.

The fox squealed as if blaming us before dashing off somewhere into the woods.

"Mgh." Ruti was displeased. I guess she wanted to look at the fox more since it was cute. She glared at the tree that had dropped the snow for a second before stomping her foot. The tremor shook all the branches around us, sending a bunch of snow falling to the ground. As a spray of white floated in the air, all sorts of little animals popped out of hiding to run away. When everything quieted down again, Ruti glanced at me with a troubled expression.

"I was just trying to knock off the snow so it wouldn't fall anymore…"

"It's fine. They'll be back as soon as we leave," I assured her as I patted her shoulder.

Ruti stared at the empty forest with obvious regret.

We continued our hike until noon. The sky overhead was blue, and the snow underfoot glimmered in the sun.

"What do you think? About time for lunch?" I asked.

"Yeah!" Rit said with a clap. "I was just starting to get hungry."

"Trudging through the snow can really drain your stamina," I remarked.

We didn't stop to set up camp until dinnertime; thus our meal needed to be something that didn't require too much preparation.

"O spirit of flame, my hand is thy stage. Dance, dance… Heat Hands."

With Rit's magic, the water in the pot started to bubble. I put in finely cut vegetables, some fresh mushrooms from the zoogs, and some bacon.

"Let it boil a bit, and then right at the end, break up some crackers and add them," I instructed.

Before departing Zoltan, I had pasted the crackers with olive oil and spices, so just dropping them into the soup would give it a little flavor. It was a matter of preference whether you ate them while they were still crispy or let them heat up until they were softer. This time I served the broth up while they were firm.

"""""Thanks for the food."""""

It was a simple meal, but it was delicious when eaten beneath the vast azure sky from a place with such a beautiful view.

"It's good, the scenery's great, and the cool mountain breeze makes the warm soup taste all the better. I'm glad I came, Red," Rit said.

Admittedly, the sentiment was a bit out of place for a perilous adventure.

"Yeah, me too."

However, it was a perfect fit for our trip.

*   *   *

My name is Tisse, and I'm a member of the Assassins Guild. Currently, I'm just an average person taking it easy in Zoltan.

I'm honestly not sure how much longer I should claim to be a part of that organization, though.

The spider riding on my hand is my partner, Mister Crawly Wawly. The *Mister* is part of his name.

"Well then, what do we do now?" Mistorm muttered to herself.

I really needed to stop playing with Mister Crawly Wawly and deal with what was happening.

"Treshpasshshersh!"

A ratlike monster up in the trees was pointing a spear at us.

"Wait, we're friends of Red's." Godwin was trying his best to explain things, but the zoogs showed no sign of letting down their guard. "Dammit! If only the horses hadn't stopped listening to us," he cursed.

The original plan had been for us to catch up on horseback and join Ruti and the others at this village last night. Unfortunately, our mounts had grown restless as we approached the Wall at the End of the World, eventually refusing to take a step closer.

We tried everything we could to get them to move, but they seemed to be spooked by something and held fast in their refusal. I did my best to bring them to a nearby settlement, intending to pay for their stabling. The village was up in arms, however, because goblins were stealing its vegetables and livestock, so I had to chase after the goblins, defeat them, and bring back what had been stolen before I could finally leave our horses and hurry back.

I'd dealt with a lot today, and I was proud of myself.

Mister Crawly Wawly patted my head with his little leg.

"Red's the only one they know, so they aren't gonna trust us," Godwin stated with a shrug. No matter what he tried, the monsters responded with hostility. "Didn't you claim you could handle this, Master Mistorm?"

"I thought so, since I had come here once before about thirty years ago. Unfortunately, I hadn't accounted for the fact that zoogs' life spans are generally only about three decades," she answered.

I had heard that Ruti and the others intended to stop here for directions to the gem giant village, but I hadn't the faintest notion where their journey had taken them after that. Yarandrala and I could probably manage to track them, but given their lead, catching up while making sure not to lose the trail would be difficult.

Our reaching Ruti's group required the zoogs telling us where they had gone. Regrettably...

"Shu shu! If you turn back, we'll leave you be, but there will be no mershy if you prosheed further!"

Even Godwin was capable of wiping out the zoogs by himself, so they were no challenge for us. And we could always get the information by catching a zoog and forcing it to take a truth serum. They were Red's friends, however. I wouldn't allow such a violent response.

Noticing my gaze, Godwin forced a wry chuckle. "I know, I know. Besides, it's not like I've got some big reason to go chasing after them anyway."

"Hmph." Yarandrala fixed him with an icy glare.

Godwin hurriedly amended his statement, wiping cold sweat from his brow. "Ah, I mean, I'll obviously still do my best to find them, though."

The man had once been a top-class criminal in Zoltan, but I couldn't shake the sense that he gave off a bootlicking air.

"Anyway, they look ready to strike at any moment. I don't suppose you have any ideas? My disarming small talk has about reached its limits, and I don't think I can stall for much longer," admitted Godwin.

Yarandrala raised an eyebrow. "Small talk?"

"Urk. I was just joking; no need to get so bent out of shape."

Godwin had grown more relaxed during our trip. Ever since being taken away to the ancient elf ruins by Ruti, he'd been dragged into all sorts of things without much choice, so I felt a little bit bad for him. He was proving to be more resilient than I'd assumed.

Just then, Yarandrala spoke up after having checked the surroundings.

"Have there been any trees falling or branches that shouldn't have broken breaking lately?"

"Shu shu!"

Hushed words rippled through the crowd of zoogs.

"How did you know that?!"

"I'm a specialist when it comes to plants. A sickness has spread through this forest," Yarandrala explained.

"What?"

"Liar!"

"But the limb really did shnap."

The zoogs' will to fight was clearly waning.

"If it ish ash you shay, then what will happen?" one asked.

"I doubt it will be the end of the forest, but many trees will rot at the roots and die."

"They'll die?!"

The zoogs were badly shaken by that. They loudly chatted back and forth with one another.

"Calm yourshelvesh," a solemn voice decreed, and the creatures obeyed, frantically clearing the way. "Hail, O tree-leaf-eared one. We have not had an audienshe with a high elf shinshe my great-grandfather'sh generation."

"This is the first I've met guardians of hyphae as well," replied Yarandrala.

The old-looking zoog who appeared was probably the village elder.

"Guardiansh of hyphae ish quite an old name. It musht be difficult for high elvesh who live sho long. I became thirty-four thish year, but I'm shtarting to look forward to returning to Demish's hide and beginning my next journey," the elder said before rubbing its hands together with a smile. "O tree-leaf-eared one, what do you mean when you shay thish foresht ish disheashed?"

"The soil around here has changed rapidly over the past few months, and the plants are suffering for it. The symptoms are not yet grave, but before long, many limbs will break, and trees will begin to fall."

"Shu shu… That'sh odd."

"The foulness in the earth grows more intense the closer we get to the Wall at the End of the World. Something might be happening up in the mountains."

"I shee. Though we know of mushroomsh, we have not been given enough time in thish world to know much of the treesh. We shall do ash the high elf shaysh."

"Elder!

"They are gueshtsh now. Lower your shpearsh."

The zoogs did as it bade, bowing before the elder.

Phew, it looks like we'll be able to manage something, then, I thought with relief.

✳   ✳   ✳

Yarandrala examined the trees, Mistorm helped out with her magic, and Godwin prepared a medicine. Meanwhile, I used the information the zoogs had provided to plot a route to intercept Red and the others.

"The safer option is to catch up tomorrow. If we really hurry, we might be able to meet up by tonight, but..."

Mister Crawly Wawly shook his head.

"Yes, you're right. Traveling without setting up camp would be dangerous. Yarandrala and I would be fine, I'm sure, but Mistorm is quite old. Making her and Godwin hike out on a mountain at night during winter is a bad idea."

The safer option was superior.

"Does that mean we won't reach them today?" Yarandrala asked from behind me.

"Yes. If we forced the matter and continued across the mountain through the evening, we might find them, but if we didn't, it would mean setting up camp late at night, and there's also a chance we'd pass them in the dark without realizing it," I explained.

"I agree. The plan to locate them tomorrow will be fine." Yarandrala nodded as she sat next to me.

"Have you finished examining the trees?" I inquired.

"The more necessary treatments have been taken care of. It went quickly, thanks to Mistorm's help. All that remains is for Godwin to finish the medicine, and we can go."

"I see."

Evidently, we would be able to leave about twenty minutes earlier than I had planned.

"Say," Yarandrala abruptly began.

"Yes?"

"My goal is to reunite with Red and Rit. Mistorm's is to meet up with Mogrim and help him, and Godwin's coming along because Mistorm told him to. She seems to be working out a way to wipe his slate clean."

"I see."

"So then what about you?"

"I'm serving as a guide."

"Had you told us that Red and the others had made for the zoog village, you wouldn't have needed to lead us, right? And from here we'll be following the trail the zoogs set us on. It seems like there's no reason for you to accompany us."

"Am I getting in the way by being here?" I asked.

"I didn't mean it like that at all!" Yarandrala insisted. I was surprised at how vehemently she denied it. Her face was deadly serious as she continued. "I'm grateful for the assistance you've provided. I don't think you've been a hindrance in the slightest. If it came across like that, then I apologize for not expressing myself clearly. I was just curious why you were going to such lengths."

"There's no need to be sorry. I wasn't particularly bothered."

Yarandrala and I had fought the day before. I doubt she trusted me yet, but judging by her reaction, she didn't seem to hold me in poor respect.

Admittedly, I wasn't being entirely honest with her. I had failed to mention that Ruti was with Red and Rit.

Ugh, my stomach hurts...

Ruti had quit being the Hero. Even if God had foisted the role upon her, she had still abandoned the quest to save the world. I could only wonder how Yarandrala, who had been one of the Hero's companions, would react to that.

I was here in case Yarandrala responded to Ruti's decision as Theodora had. If Ruti had to fight, then I wanted to be at her side. In that sense, I didn't trust Yarandrala all that much.

"Yarandrala…"

"Yes?"

Part of my job as a member of the Assassins Guild was to probe for openings in a target that I could exploit, but this was different. I wanted to do everything I could to support my friend Ruti.

"Why did you become one of the Hero's companions?"

The high elf fixed me with her gaze. "So you know who I am."

"Because I'm friends with Red and Rit, and one other person as well," I responded.

"Which means I'm not mistaken about Red's true identity."

"Correct."

Yarandrala closed her eyes and exhaled. "…I was so sure of it, but it really is a relief to have some confirmation. Thank goodness. He truly is still alive."

I had heard that Yarandrala feared Ares might have killed Red. Searching for news of a potentially slain comrade must have been demoralizing.

"I'm sorry. You wanted to know why I joined the Hero, right?"

"Yes."

"It's simple. My cherished friend Gideon—Red—was in that party."

"That's all?" I pressed.

"Yes, that's all. I would have liked to save the world, too, if we could manage that, and I wished to help people who were suffering. But if that was all I'd aspired to, I could have joined the army. Choosing to attempt to defeat the demon lord with six people is absurd."

I was stunned by Yarandrala's candid statement. "Absurd?!"

"Yes, that's the best word to describe it. Why did we intentionally fight with so few people?"

"To employ the Hero's ultimate battle strength as the core of the party while maximizing mobility. In fact, the Avalon allied army successfully mounted a counterattack as the Hero grew in strength to fight the demon lord's forces."

"But that's just because the Hero continued to win. She carries the world on her shoulders, and if she ever falls, all of those plans will collapse. That's the sort of foolish gamble the Hero's existence is."

That's...

Red and Ares had always given the impression that Yarandrala was a kindly older sister with a capricious streak. Yet the woman speaking now held no illusions about Ruti.

"Hero is indeed the most powerful blessing in the world. And it may seem that its bearer is acting in the best interests of the world because of the blessing's impulses. However, that assumption of what is best includes the added expectation that the Hero will bear everything alone. The best response would be to deploy an army with the Hero. Not some improvised thrown-together horde, but a proper, trained force with the Hero as the commander. There is no reason for the Hero to fight at the front. She should be at the rear to put the troops at ease and grant them courage."

"Red never mentioned you having that sort of opinion," I admitted.

"Mentioning as much to him would only cause him needless pain. Besides, he understood it as well as I. Sadly, the Hero's impulses would not allow that choice because the Hero blessing never takes its bearer's life into account. That is surely why God provided the Guide to protect the Hero."

"So...would you say that there is no need for the Hero to continue fighting for the sake of the world?"

"Hmmm...I see..." Yarandrala stared at me for a moment. "You don't need to worry about that. I'm on Red's side... Still, that's quite a surprise," Yarandrala admitted with a laugh. "I hadn't expected Ruti to be here as well!"

This high elf woman seemed far more hot-tempered, far more cool-headed, far sharper, and far kinder than I had imagined.

Chapter 4

- - - - - - - - -

Reuniting with Yarandrala

That morning in the forest, a large figure and a small one were fighting. The former was a monster called a rock troll, a two-meter-tall humanoid creature with a thick skin as hard as a stone. The rock troll held a club in its right hand and bared its fangs to intimidate its opponent. Its weapon was made of lead instead of iron, which was odd.

The monster was engaged with Mogrim. He was edging closer, ax in hand. "Raaaah!" he roared as he leaped onto the rock troll and slammed his weapon down. The ax Mogrim had forged himself easily split the troll's rocklike skin, and it fell with a pained cry.

"Ha-ha! Didjya see that?!" Mogrim shouted, waving his weapon around. To be honest, there probably weren't many adventurers in Zoltan who could defeat a rock troll.

"I thought you might have a little trouble fighting since your blessing is more craft oriented, but you're stronger than I would have guessed," I conceded.

"Wa-ha-ha! 'Cause I've got no talent for any of that magic stuff! I gave up on it and poured everything into forging and combat skills! Watch this! Throwing Mastery: Ricochet Toss!"

Mogrim hurled his ax at the monster, and it bounced off.

"Graargh!" a rock troll's dying cry filled the air. The rebounding ax had arced and hit another rock troll that was hiding nearby and taking aim at us.

"Wa-ha-ha! They don't call me the drake slayer for nothing!"

"Uh-huh. You might really have managed to kill a drake," I said.

"So you finally believe me!"

Mogrim guffawed exuberantly as he pulled his weapon out of the back of the fallen monster. At this rate, he was liable to launch into another one of his stories, so I hurriedly clapped my hands.

"That was the last one. Let's keep moving," I urged.

"Yeah, a drake slayer like me— Wait, what were we doing?"

"The drake slayer's job is gathering firewood," I stated, gesturing to the logs I was carrying on my back.

✳   ✳   ✳

"Welcome back."

By the time Mogrim and I returned to the meeting point, Rit and Ruti were waiting for us.

"Looks like you two gathered a good amount," I remarked.

"Yeah, about three days' worth. Not bad for just an hour's work," Rit replied.

"We gave it our all," appended Ruti.

Mogrim and I had only gotten about two days' worth, but we had also run into a group of rock trolls.

"See, this is what happens when you get caught battling monsters, Mogrim."

"I—I mean, they were all around us. What was I gonna do, leave them alone? Plus, you were the one saying there was no telling when they might try to attack us."

The dwarf tried to shift the blame as we set our gathered firewood down.

"That's about five days between us. The plan was to reach the gem giants' village tomorrow, though," Rit stated.

"Yeah, but this is as high as the land can support forest growth. We won't be able to gather any more firewood past this point."

I tied up the logs and packed it away into my backpack. One day's worth weighed about seven kilograms, bringing the load to thirty-five for five days. It would have been nice to use an item box, but they registered each log individually, which meant imagining each one when retrieving them later. It was challenging to recall every piece in a large bundle, and it wasn't that uncommon to forget and not be able to get everything out, so for consumables like this, the surer thing was to lug them like normal.

"All right, shall we be off?" I asked.

"Yeah! It's nice weather today! This is turning out to be a pretty nice trip!" Rit exclaimed as she looked upward.

The sky was breathtakingly clear, and there was a gentle breeze blowing. It had threatened to snow last night, but we'd gotten lucky. Today was even warmer than we'd expected. Rit was right to say this journey was proving very enjoyable.

Beyond the forest line, the scenery changed.

Without trees to block the view, we could see far off into the distance in all directions. The sky especially felt wider and closer. Overhead, there was nothing but blue.

"Okay," I said with resolve.

"Hmm? What is it?" Rit questioned. Then I plopped down on my back and gazed at the heavens.

"Eh? Uh? Are you okay?!"

"The sky is gorgeous."

"Ah-ha-ha. Ohhhh." Rit laughed and then sat down next to me. "It does feel nice to sit and watch it."

"Right?"

"What in blazes are you two doing? You realize this is the Wall at the End of the World, right? The great mountain range feared by all travelers?" Mogrim questioned with a dumbfounded chuckle.

"We've come all this way, and it's not like you have a lot of opportunities to see sights like this, so it'd be a waste not to enjoy the scenery, don't you think?" I argued.

"I can't say there's not some logic to that, but—"

"You and Ruti should try lying down like this, too. The grass doesn't feel bad, either...?" I trailed off. Something odd had caught my attention.

Is the ground shaking?

"What is it, Red?" asked Mogrim.

"It's just it sort of felt like the ground was shaking a little bit."

"An earthquake?"

"It felt different from that."

Mogrim's face went pale, and he put his ear to the ground. Then Ruti looked up at the mountain with a grim expression.

"Is it an avalanche?!" the dwarf cried.

I shook my head. "No, there's not enough snow for an avalanche... This is..."

We leaped to our feet. The ground seemed to be melting farther up the mountain, like a wax sculpture held to flame.

"It's a landslide!" I exclaimed.

A plume of dirt whipped up into the air as the wave of sediment bore down on us like a dragon hunting its prey.

"Wh-what do we do?!" Mogrim shouted.

"Rit!" I called.

"No. I can only maintain my Levitate for a few minutes, and the flight speed is slower than walking. I can't get us all out of the path."

"Forget me! I'm sure y'all can do something to take care of yourselves!"

Rit grimaced at Mogrim's words.

Ruti, however, kept her calm. She grabbed Mogrim and Rit. "A few minutes is enough."

"Eh? Ah? Aaaaaaaaaaaaaaah!!!"

Ruti hurled the two of them about a hundred meters into the air.

"As for me—" Ruti hopped into my arms. "We can escape using your Lightning Speed."

I started sprinting, cradling Ruti in my arms like a princess.

"I'm the lightest of the three of us, so this is the logical choice. Mhm." My sister looked extremely satisfied as she wrapped her arms around my neck while I dashed out of the path of the landslide.

The dirt and rock buried the grassy field as it passed. Yet even that violence, that terrifying sound, died into silence after a mere ten minutes.

I breathed a sigh of relief as I lowered Ruti to the ground.

"It's over now."

Curiously, Ruti looked a bit disappointed. Looking around, I saw that Rit and Mogrim had made it to a spot with higher elevation.

"There they are. Looks like they're okay," I observed with relief, sighing.

"Are you okay, Big Brother?"

"Yeah, just a little tired is all."

"Tired? But you shouldn't be able to get worn out."

"Normally, yeah. But being high on a mountain isn't really a typical situation."

Ordinarily, Lightning Speed demanded tremendous amounts of stamina. I compensated for that with Immunity to Fatigue, but that wasn't enough to cover it with the thinner air up here.

"It's nothing too bad," I assured her. "It's just been a while since I felt a little exhausted, so I was surprised."

"Okay. Next time I'll carry you, then," Ruti decided.

"Hmm? Okay, if the time comes, I'll be counting on you."

"Please do."

Ruti looked to be in a good mood as we made our way to Rit and Mogrim. Fortunately, neither of them appeared injured.

"Are you two all right?" I asked.

Rit nodded. "Yeah, just a little surprised."

"I'm a lot more than just a little surprised! What kinda arm strength do you have to throw us that kind of distance?" Mogrim yelled.

"I made sure to control it so you didn't fly too far," Ruti stated flatly.

"Wait, that wasn't even full strength?!"

"My Ruti's amazing, isn't she?"

"Why are you bragging?"

"Because she's my sister."

"Yeah, I'm Big Brother's sister."

Mogrim was at a loss for words as he looked at Ruti, while Rit just shrugged and laughed.

"Okay, now that we know everyone's safe, I'd like to keep heading up, but…" I stopped there to have a look around.

The landslide had left a trail of mud and rocks of all shapes and sizes in its wake. Walking through that would be a challenge.

"I guess we'll take a detour."

✳   ✳   ✳

We found the traces of their camp before noon. The blackened firewood was still warm to the touch.

"It's been at least ten years since I came out this far, but the scenery's still just as breathtaking. What do you think, Yarandrala? Nice view, isn't it?" Mistorm asked as she turned to survey things behind.

I didn't bother to look back, though.

"I'll enjoy the vista after I've met with Red and the others," I replied.

"I see."

I continued pressing forward. I was aware that my tone was sharp, and I knew full well it was upsetting the party's mood. However, since we'd started hiking through the mountains, I'd been gripped by a sense of unease. The foliage was cowering.

Something was happening on these peaks. I had no clue what was scaring the plants, but I was worried for their safety.

"You guys sure are tough," Godwin remarked as he brought up the rear. "We've been attacked by rock trolls, what, five times since this morning? I'm beat."

"We left while it was still dark, so that was bound to happen," I responded.

As a general rule, monsters were more active at night. Rock trolls could see in the dark, so they were right at home from dusk until dawn.

"Still, that's the first time I've seen a rock troll with a lead club," Mistorm muttered.

Rock trolls were fairly primitive beings, but they were capable of building small furnaces and tempering iron. Perhaps out of pride in their tough skin, they did not craft armor or shields. Instead, they focused on clubs, throwing spears, and other weapons that suited their powerful arms.

I had never heard of them creating armaments from lead before, either. Perhaps some other monsters were keeping the trolls away from the iron veins they typically used.

"Red, Rit, Ruti…"

I knew how capable each of them was. They weren't the sort to be caught unawares, but…

"I'm going to pick up the pace a little bit," I decided.

"Wait, really?" Despite his complaint, Godwin matched my speed. Tisse silently sped up as well. She had been largely silent during our trip. Mistorm didn't fall behind, either, muttering, "Dearie me" and shaking her head. For a woman old enough to rely on a walking stick, that was no trivial feat.

The boots Mistorm was wearing had been made by a dwarf. They were likely enchanted to decrease stamina consumption.

Everyone's doing well to keep moving… I really should apologize once we meet up with Red's group. But for now, I hope they'll excuse my selfish and haughty high elf behavior for a little longer.

After we pushed on for a while, there was an audible tremor from farther up the mountain.

"It's a landslide. It won't hit us directly, but there is a chance the rocks and dirt will cross our route," Tisse said.

"Oh, I've never seen a landslide for myself before," Godwin offered.

We pulled back a bit, and before long, the wave of soil passed with a thundering sound. Our trail was buried in dirt and stone. It was fortunate we'd left the path when we had.

"Well, ain't that a mess."

Mistorm was right. The slope of the peak we were trying to climb was blanketed in loose earth and rock.

Godwin looked pale. "Wait a minute, what about Red and the others? They're ahead of us, right?"

"It's okay," Tisse assured him, her expression unchanged as she touched the ground. "There's no trace of anyone buried."

"You can tell something like that?" Godwin questioned.

"I can. Sensing presences is a specialty of mine."

"I checked with my magic, too. There isn't anyone I know beneath the surface," Mistorm assured.

"The plants confirm the same," I added.

"...Well, aren't you guys handy to have around," Godwin said with a sniff.

Red and the others were heroes who had battled the demon lord's army. Mistorm had compared me to a hurricane, but if anyone could stop something like a landslide, they could.

"This is rather problematic, however," Tisse remarked.

"What do you mean?" Godwin questioned.

"We don't know how they avoided the landslide or where they may have detoured," she responded.

I took a step out into the churned soil.

Godwin gawked at the action. "W-wait a sec. You're gonna walk through that? Finding a way around has to be a better choice, right?"

"If we do, we'll lose their trail. Let's continue," I said.

"But look at the path..." Godwin looked nervous. It was undoubtedly dangerous to march through the wake of a landslide. Mistorm seemed to be mulling something over.

"You can communicate with plants, right?" she asked.

"Yes, as you've seen."

"How exactly do plants see things?"

"It's difficult to express in words. Perhaps it would be closest to say that they detect the flow of the atmosphere and mana."

"I see. Then if I conjured a spirit raven, we should be able to have it carry one of your plants up into the air to scout from above. I can only maintain my summon for about ten minutes, but we might find some clues about the path Red and the others took around this."

"That's an excellent idea. Thank you!"

I believed that Red and his companions were okay, but I couldn't shake my anxiousness, the uncertainty of what if, so I was genuinely grateful for Mistorm's suggestion.

"Heed my call, O sable-winged friend, and hasten thy flight. Summon Spirit Raven."

Mistorm signed a seal, and a raven appeared on her shoulder. The summoned bird cawed at me and stuck out its left leg. I entwined a small berry vine around it.

"Go."

"Caaw!"

At its master's instruction, the raven took off. Spreading its wings, it rode the wind in a wide spiral, rising to a high altitude before slowly gliding out in the direction of the summit. I closed my eyes and focused my senses on the vine around its leg.

The world that plants saw was one of vitality. Yet in the wreckage of the landslide, the scene was one of life fading. Countless lives lost or dimming. It was a distressing scene, and I could feel the burden growing on my heart. Still, I scoured the wasteland.

And then my eyes snapped open.

"He's there!"

I started running immediately.

"W-wait!"

Godwin tried to call me back, but I wasn't going to stop. I hurried through the mud without any concern for my clothes or shoes, grabbing rocks to pull myself forward despite cutting my fingers. I cut diagonally across the swath of the landslide's destruction and climbed

a slope where small white flowers were growing. The hill would have provided an excellent refuge for anyone caught in the deluge of earth—an island of soft grass amid mud and stone.

I frantically sprinted the last hundred meters to the top of the mound, and there he was. He was lying comfortably on the ground, eyes wide as he looked at me.

He was still alive. I had finally found him again.

"Gideon!!!"

I should have said Red, but I couldn't help myself. The name flew from my lips before I understood I was speaking it.

*   *   *

I was shocked at the wholly unexpected reunion with Yarandrala. Fortunately, Tisse, who had accompanied my old friend, helped to smooth things over. Plans being what they were, we decided to keep moving until evening, when we would set up camp and have a real conversation.

Tisse and Godwin intended to accompany us until morning, when they would return to Zoltan.

With Mistorm and the others around, Yarandrala and I couldn't discuss what had happened after I left the party, but thankfully, she seemed to understand that. She hadn't probed at all while we were walking together.

Currently, she and I were sitting across from each other at the campfire.

"I always thought our reunion would be more dramatic than this," Yarandrala admitted quietly.

The tripod and a small pot of water were sitting over the fire.

"Dramatic how? I definitely wasn't expecting to see you here," I replied.

"Like...you showing up while I'm fighting a horde of dragons. Or battling back-to-back against the demon lord's army!"

"Ah-ha-ha. Yeah, I think I'll pass on that."

"Hee-hee. You've always been that way, though. Remember when we met in Loggervia? When I was fighting the demon lord's army there?"

"I was shocked when I heard you were in Loggervia. And I will admit I did rush over to help. But I couldn't help the villagers get to safety, so I wound up having to leave everything to you and go back."

"That just means you trusted me, right? Loggervia is so far from the capital, yet you still came to save me... I was thrilled."

"Calling the whole thing fortunate seems wrong since the village where your friends lived was under attack, but yeah, I can't deny it was dramatic."

Yarandrala's strength had been decisive during Loggervia's counter-attack; her guiding us through the bewitching woods that were thought impassable had allowed us to break through the enemy's siege and plead for help from neighboring countries. There's no telling what would have transpired had Yarandrala not been there.

"This time, however, you were taking a nap and enjoying the view when I found you," the high elf said.

"We stopped to enjoy the view in a very conspicuous and clear spot. It's not astonishing you happened upon us when you did," I replied. Yarandrala poured a cup of tea from the pot. I paused to enjoy the fragrance as I took a sip. "Amazing as always."

Yarandrala's evening tea had just a hint of bitterness and left a refreshing sensation. It was a very relaxing flavor. The tea leaves had been blended with several herbs, just a few of many that Yarandrala carried on her.

"I've always sought to match this flavor," I remarked.

"It's a blend I've been crafting all my life. Even if you are my favorite pupil, it will still take you at least eighty years to figure it out."

"Eighty years, huh? That's so long."

"It will pass before you know it."

Yarandrala sipped from her own cup and then exhaled a white puff that drifted into the cool night air.

"Picking up where we left off there...," she began.

I cocked my head to one side. "Hmm?"

"I'm glad I could have such a tranquil reunion with you."

"Ah...yeah. Enjoying tea in peace is nice."

"You've always been fighting, heroically determined to set out on a journey to save the world someday. I bet the old you never would have been able to imagine such an idyllic reunion."

"Back then, I spent every waking moment battling, trying to get even the tiniest bit stronger. If we were to meet again, it would have been dramatic, in the middle of combat... You're right, I probably wouldn't have thought something like this possible."

"Yet here we are in such a calm setting. I always wanted you and Rit to live for yourselves. To enjoy the sort of life where you could exist happily with the person you love."

"Yarandrala..."

Her face looked beautiful in the fire's glow.

High elves possessed well-proportioned features, but Yarandrala's wild and free expression darkened with shadows of grief and loneliness from time to time. To me, that allure was Yarandrala's alone, something altogether different from the flawless beauty of her kin.

By my own estimation, Yarandrala was fairly old, even for a high elf. I had never heard an actual number, but it had to be greater than one hundred. She had run away from Kiramin at a young age and spent several decades as an adventurer. After all her old companions fell in combat or died of old age, she retired. While she visited Kiramin occasionally, Yarandrala had elected to continue living in human society.

The other name for high elves was urban elves, and, true to that name, they had a tendency to gather in a single town or group. Yarandrala was likely a bit of an odd case among high elves, but that was part of her unique charm.

If things had been different... If I had been a little more aware of what was going on around me back when I was in the capital, maybe...

"If we had met under different circumstances, do you think we might have ended up together?"

Yarandrala's sudden question put me at a loss for words. After a moment, however, I shook my head and brushed the ponderings aside.

In the end, so long as I was still myself, no matter how many lives I lived, I still would have prioritized guarding Ruti. That had led to my meeting Rit and leaving her in Loggervia, getting pushed out of the party by Ares, and finding Rit in Zoltan. It was going through everything that had made me ready to settle down for a peaceful life.

I don't think I could have lived any differently.

"Probably not," I replied.

"Yeah."

Before I realized it, my cup had run dry, and Yarandrala was pouring me a new one.

"That's for the best. Having to watch someone I love die right before my eyes again would be awful. I'll be praying for your happiness, and when the day comes for us to part ways, we can do so amicably."

"I'm still working on proposing to Rit, and you're already worrying about farewells?"

"Humans live their lives in such a rush. If I stop to look around a bit, they vanish," Yarandrala said.

"Like children growing up."

"Indeed, just like children. And yet, from time to time, there are moments when they can seem so much more mature than I with all the years I've lived. A glimpse of wisdom that dwarves and orcs don't ever exhibit. That is probably why we high elves are capable of falling in love with humans."

Yarandrala leaned in to peer at my face. Getting a little bit embarrassed, I glanced away. Her cheerful laugh sang in my ear.

"Red's given my tea high praise, so would the two of you like to try it?" Yarandrala called.

There was a rustle in the underbrush as Rit and Ruti peeked out from the shadows.

"Eh-heh-heh. Caught us, huh?" asked the former.

"I couldn't trick the plants," the latter stated.

"Indeed. Even if you deceive me, you cannot fool my friends. So don't sit out there in the cold. Come here and have some warm tea."

Rit and Ruti sat down next to me as Yarandrala got two more cups and filled them. Then she removed the tea leaves from the empty pot and added some fresh ones and hot water.

"I'm sure you'll want a second cup," the high elf said confidently.

Ruti and Rit each sampled the brew.

"Delicious… This is sort of like the tea that Big Brother makes."

"Yeah, Red makes a kind with a similar taste."

"Hee-hee. Naturally, since I'm the one who taught him how to make it."

Rit took another sip and nodded, while Ruti partook of hers much quicker, evidently enjoying the flavor. A kindly smile crossed Yarandrala's lips as she watched.

"Ruti, do you like my tea?"

"Mhm. It's delicious—just like Big Brother's."

"I've made tea for you before when we were traveling together," Yarandrala recalled.

"Mhm, I know. But back then, I…" Ruti trailed off, looking troubled.

The Hero blessing's many immunities and resistances had heightened Ruti's sense of taste to enable her to detect the slightest trace of poison. In exchange, she had grown incredibly numb to typical flavors. What's more, she was always in peak condition and never required food. Thus, while she had been able to recognize the taste of tea, she'd never understood it as being delicious.

Seeing that Ruti was troubled, I tried to explain, but Yarandrala gently stopped me.

"I'm glad you're finally able to say you enjoy my tea, Ruti. It feels like we've finally become friends."

"Friends?" Ruti questioned.

Yarandrala nodded. "The Hero and I trusted each other, but you couldn't describe our relationship as amicable. But things are different now, right?"

"Mhm."

"That's why I'm glad. I like you how you are now."

High elves weren't the sort to open up to just anyone, but once they did let someone in, they expressed their affection physically. Yarandrala softly embraced Ruti and laughed melodically.

"I have a proposition for the three of you," she said.

"What is it?" I inquired.

Still hugging Ruti close, Yarandrala answered, "Would you like to move to Kiramin with me?"

Rit and I were shocked.

"Delicious."

Ruti, however, was unmoved, standing there in Yarandrala's embrace as she drank the tea.

*   *   *

The Kingdom of Kiramin was the high elves' country, and the only nation on the continent of Avalon ruled by nonhumans that could lay rightful claim to being a kingdom.

"The weather in Kiramin is similar to Loggervia. It's a city-state established in the cold northern plains. Magic keeps the weather springlike within Kiramin's borders. It's the largest settlement on the continent—a beautiful place inhabited by countless high elves and their friends. The great temple is studded with crystals, and the inner sanctum rivals the Last Wall fortress. Kiramin's walls are constructed from eternal boulders and are an absolute defense against frost giant invasions," Yarandrala detailed, taking Rit's hand and mine. "High elves are by no means perfect—they have their share of flaws. And Kiramin isn't some utopian paradise, but...we will never betray you."

"W-wait a minute there. Could you elaborate a bit? We've hardly spoken about what's happened to us since we last met," I said.

"You were betrayed by Ares and pushed out of the party, and no one even attempted to find you," Yarandrala summarized.

"That's…"

"And as for you, Rit, you saved Loggervia. You fought countless battles for your homeland, lost your master and comrades, but still battled to the bitter end. Yet despite all your efforts, you wound up leaving Loggervia alone."

Yarandrala's grip tightened on my hand. She probably did the same with Rit's, too.

"H-hold on. I did leave Loggervia, but I was the one who suggested it. That wasn't anyone else's fault."

Rit was the hero who had saved her homeland. Even during the reconstruction after the fighting, she had given her all for the sake of the Duchy of Loggervia, using both her royal authority and everything she knew about the townsfolk from her time as an adventurer. Her endeavors had given hope to the people, from the lowest rungs up to the nobility.

There was nothing wrong with that, of course, but she had gotten too famous—she was too heroic. Some had started to wonder if she was better suited to rule than the current successor. The idea quietly began to spread throughout all of Loggervian society.

"My younger brother had already been chosen to be crowned the next king, and I didn't want to get in the way. That's all," Rit stated.

"I wouldn't have let you set off alone like that. Were it up to me, you would have been allowed to remain in your homeland, no matter what rules needed to be bent. Just as you saved Loggervia, your country should have saved you. That's the high elf perspective on the matter, anyway."

"Yarandrala…"

There were tears in Yarandrala's eyes. She looked heartbroken.

"From the very beginning, Red always did everything he could for the party. Yet no one bothered to look for him."

"It got to a point where I couldn't keep up in battle anymore. Ares certainly had his own agenda, but I definitely saw logic in his decision. So I don't think Theodora or Danan can be blamed for not immediately chasing after me," I said.

"Can't be blamed?! Not you, too!"

Yarandrala drew so close, our faces were almost touching.

"I—I only mean that I don't think less of them…"

"Even if you really had become just a hindrance, I wanted to travel together with you! If you were suffering, I wanted you to lean on me! To cast aside someone who supported you for so long just because he stopped being useful? I can't accept that! I don't want to! We were comrades, weren't we?!" The high elf's response was so earnest and heartfelt that I was at a loss for what to say. "I would never betray you."

This was how Yarandrala genuinely felt. It was such a mass of emotion that I didn't know how to respond.

Rit spoke up in my stead. "But, Yarandrala…"

"Are you going to tell me they're guiltless for what they did to him, too?"

"No, on that point, at least, I completely agree with you. No matter how much Red might think otherwise, I can't forgive that. They were absolutely wrong to cast him out."

Huh?

"I knew you'd understand!"

"Of course!"

"Umm, Rit?"

I hadn't anticipated her taking Yarandrala's side. The two of them bore down on me, pressing against me until I was about to fall over. Yet before I could, Ruti pushed up against my back.

"I'll support you, Big Brother."

"Uh, ummm."

Rit and Yarandrala were shoving me from the front while Ruti was clinging and supporting me behind.

"W-wait, you're all a little close…," I protested feebly.

Hemmed in on all sides by three beautiful young ladies—Yarandrala looked like a young lady at least, even if she was technically getting up there—I started to falter.

"Anyway, when we get back to Zoltan, we can explore in detail just how much you helped the party and just how wrong Ares was to push you away."

"Uh, yeah."

"Look, Yarandrala." Rit turned her attention from me to the high elf. "You are right that forcing him out was wrong. And yeah, maybe Loggervia should have done more to accommodate me. But even so, we aren't going to go to Kiramin."

"Why?"

"Because we're happy living here in Zoltan," Rit stated bluntly. "If you had found Red right after he had been pushed out, or me right after I left Loggervia, or Ruti before she reunited with Red, then we probably would have gone with you. But we've already made a home for ourselves here. Right, Red?" Rit smiled at me.

That expression was always so stunning.

"Yep, Rit's right. I have a great life here in Zoltan. For the first time, I'm living for myself. The same goes for Rit, Ruti, Tisse, Mogrim, Mistorm, Gonz, Tanta, Nao, Mido, Al, Dr. Newman, the craftsman Stormthunder, Mink, Oparara, Moen, and even Godwin. They're all living for themselves. I have lots of friends in Zoltan, and I'm glad to reside there. The original reason I chose Zoltan was that it was a place where I could live in peace without worrying about anyone discovering my true identity. Still, it's grown on me, and I want to spend my days there."

Yarandrala still looked unsure. "...But you might get betrayed again..."

"That's true. There's no guarantee we won't be wronged again. Our friends in Zoltan aren't heroes by any means. They're just normal people. I doubt they'd be willing to maintain their friendship no matter what the cost if it came to that."

"Then you should come with me!" Yarandrala pleaded.

"Our current friendships and happiness are still real, however."

This time Yarandrala fumbled with how to reply.

"When someone waves me down in the evening and suggests going for a drink, if I say I can't go without Rit and Ruti and them, they'll tease me for it, but they immediately suggest we have a family dinner party. I'm plenty happy with that kind of relationship."

"I'm just...worried you'll get hurt..."

"I know. I never expected you to accept this right away," I responded. "So how about you stick around in Zoltan with us for a little while?"

"Eh?"

"There's no real rush for us to head to Kiramin, right? Why don't you wait to decide? That way, you can spend some time with us and see the sort of lives we have in Zoltan."

"...Hee-hee..." Yarandrala giggled gently. "The old you would have chosen on the spot. You used to be so vehement about how bad it was to put things off."

"Different times call for different measures. And, well, I've grown more open to a relaxed pace."

"Humans keep changing by leaps and bounds. I'm always getting left behind."

Yarandrala placed her hands on my cheeks.

"Okay, we can return to this discussion later. In exchange, I'll stay here in Zoltan for a time. Does that work for you?"

"Fine by me."

Yarandrala and I both grinned.

That reminds me, we used to get into arguments from time to time back in the capital.

"This conversation is done."

Ruti pulled me backward, and Yarandrala's fingers left my cheeks. Ruti kept hugging me, still a bit annoyed.

"The answer was obvious from the start anyway," Ruti muttered.

She had a point. Were it only Rit and I, that would have been one thing, but Ruti was with us. Unlike tiny little Zoltan out on the frontier, Kiramin was a vital member of the allied forces. If the Hero was there, it would weigh heavily on the power balance among the allies. There would be no way to maintain an easy, slow life like that.

"Yeah," I said as I caressed Ruti's head.

Her eyes narrowed happily as she leaned against me.

Our decision was already made. If Ruti couldn't go to Kiramin, then I wouldn't be leaving Zoltan.

"Have you finished your conversation?"

"Wah?!"

A small figure appeared from the darkness. Rit and I were obviously surprised, but even Yarandrala was caught off guard despite her ability to detect invisible beings through the surrounding plants. The only one unmoved was Ruti.

"T-Tisse, don't scare me like that," Yarandrala insisted.

"My apologies," she responded, her expression unchanged. No, there was the slightest trace of an impatient air to her.

Perhaps this was her way of getting some revenge on Yarandrala.

"Then next up is my business," Tisse stated.

"Your business?" I questioned, glancing over at Yarandrala. Even though they had come out here together, she didn't seem to know what Tisse was talking about, either.

Tisse slapped a handmade chart down in front of us.

"What's this?" I inquired.

"It's a map put together using all the information I gathered from the zoogs."

I looked the chart over. "Hooo, it's pretty filled out, even down to the gem giants' village. So what is this symbol marking?"

"A hot spring."

"Ah."

Right, that rumor about a hot spring at the Wall at the End of the World. Tisse had evidently managed to get some info about it from the zoogs.

"It is about a fifteen-minute walk from here." Tisse remained expressionless as she spoke, but her eyes were gleaming.

So the reason she'd accompanied us to the camp instead of leaving once we had met up was that she wanted to visit the hot spring? Well, I imagine she was probably worried about both us and Yarandrala, but...

"We should go check it out," said Tisse.

"What?!" Yarandrala's expression lit up. "If you had critical information like that, why didn't you say anything sooner?!"

"Oh, are you also a fan of baths, Yarandrala?" Tisse questioned.

"But of course!"

Yarandrala was always a bit of a stickler for cleanliness. Even during our travels, she washed her body every day without fail, and if there was a river around, she often bathed in it. That a hot spring enticed her was no surprise.

Tisse nodded. "Then Yarandrala and I are going. How about the rest of you?"

"Count me in," Rit declared.

"If Big Brother is going, then I'll come, too," Ruti added.

Four sets of eyes fell on me.

"A hot spring, huh? I mean, I'd like to take a dip…but it's a natural one, right? It might be being maintained by monsters…" There were creatures besides humans and elves that enjoyed relaxing baths. Many natural hot springs were tended by monsters. This meant there was a caveat: "I doubt they have a divide for the men's bath and women's bath."

Monsters didn't feel shame when it came to males and females exposing themselves to each other.

"So how about you all go first, and any men who want a dip can go after," I suggested.

"Ehhh? I want to enjoy it with you, though," Rit complained.

I frowned slightly, arguing, "Yeah, but Tisse is here, too, and all."

"You don't have to mind me. I'm going to go into my own little world while enjoying the hot spring," the Assassin replied.

"Wait a minute. This isn't just me we're talking about. What about Godwin and Mogrim?" I reminded them.

"Ahh, yeah, that would be a little…," Rit admitted.

"See what I mean?" I said.

However, Rit shook her head. "We still need a lookout while we're in the hot springs. So you alone can come."

I suppose she had a point. I doubted any monsters could win against

Ruti, even if she was naked, but I'd like it if they could relax and forget about being on a mountainside crawling with dangerous monsters for a while.

"In that case…fine, I'll tag along," I conceded.

"Hooray!" cheered Rit.

"All right, you all get ready. I'm going to let Mistorm know."

It was charming seeing how excitedly Tisse and the others prepared their toiletries as I got up and headed over to Mistorm. She, Mogrim, and Godwin had sensed we were going to talk about the past and had thoughtfully set up camp out of earshot.

Heading toward the glow of the fire, I saw Mistorm sitting cross-legged on a mat and meditating.

"Is that you, Red?" she asked without opening her eyes.

Mogrim was polishing his weapons, and Godwin was eating what looked like a hard candy made from roasted sugar.

"Apparently, there's a hot spring nearby. Rit and the others were planning to go take a dip, so I came to see if you wanted to join."

"A hot spring, eh? Ah, that would be nice, but I'm currently recovering my magic power, as you can see. When you reach my age, it just doesn't come back like it used to. Once I'm done, I'm planning to go straight to bed. Thanks for the offer, but I'll have to pass."

"Okay."

I glanced over at Mogrim and Godwin.

"I'm already beat. I don't wanna take another step," Godwin groaned, turning me down.

"I love a good sauna, but I'm not much for large baths," Mogrim responded evasively.

Oh yeah, he can't swim.

"It's not like you're going to drown in a bath."

"Yeah, but humans and dwarves can't breathe underwater, either. That means we're not meant to be submerged."

"I see…"

Mogrim washed his body and kept himself clean, so I suppose it didn't much matter.

"Way back, I used to think washing my body maybe two times a week was enough," the dwarf admitted.

"That's a little too infrequent…," I remarked.

"Yeah, before long, the missus started giving me a good scrubbing every day."

"Sounds like a pet dog."

"Ha-ha-ha. A pet, huh? You're not too far off, in a way. Regardless, thanks to her, I've gotten right used to keeping clean. It's to the point where I feel off if I don't wash up," Mogrim said with a cheerful, toothy laugh.

Godwin and I joined him, and Mistorm grudgingly chuckled as well while telling us not to mess with her concentration.

"It's your fault she got mad at us, Red."

"My fault? Anyway, you've got yourself a wonderful wife."

"Damn straight. My lady's the best in the world… She's wasted on someone like me."

"She caught you trying to sneak out to gather materials, huh?"

I had heard from Mistorm that Mink had asked her to lend Mogrim a hand. He had attempted to leave without giving her reason to fret, but finding out that she knew what he was up to had made Mogrim's small, stout frame shrink in embarrassment.

"There's nothing wrong with that," I assured him, patting his back as I sat down next to him. "You were trying to do everything in your power to help Mink, and because she wanted to lend you a hand, she asked Mistorm for aid. You have a nice relationship."

"Hmm," grunted Mogrim.

"Had you been honest with Mink outright, Mistorm wouldn't have had to chase after you, but she caught up without too much trouble. I think that roundaboutness is a nice thing, too. Validating, in a way."

"…Yeah! You're right! My wife's the best!"

"You've been married for so long, but you're still hopeless romantics at heart," I remarked.

"Heh, you could learn a thing or two from us, Red."

"Yeah, yeah… We're going to be hopeless romantics, too, no matter how many years pass."

There was a loud crunch, the sound of a hard candy shattering.

"Gah! What is this conversation?! Put yourself in my shoes for a minute and have a bit of self-control!" Godwin cried.

I cocked an eyebrow. "What? Is something bothering you?"

"Is something bothering me? Damn straight something's bothering me!" Godwin threw some dirt at me. Sheesh, what an awkward guy.

Hoping to change the subject, I inquired, "Say, what are you going to do after this, Godwin?"

"I'm going back down the mountain with Tisse."

"I meant beyond that."

Godwin was a wanted man, having escaped from prison and all. Mistorm had helped him out this time, but it would be a one-way trip to the gallows if he got caught again.

"Heh-heh-heh. All that's behind me now." Godwin smirked. "The deal was I help Master Mistorm investigate the dangerous Wall at the End of the World and bring back the records of those investigations, and in exchange, she sweeps the whole Devil's Blessing thing under the rug."

"Whoa there. We're not just talking about the Zoltan judiciary here. This involves the church, too, right? Even for her..."

I glanced over at Mistorm. She had one eye open and was smirking.

"The head of the Zoltan church is an old friend of mine."

Back when Mistorm had been an adventurer, one of the members of her party had been a bishop named Shien. In the time since, he had risen to run the local sect.

"I've got enough clout to push that through," Mistorm declared.

Unsure if that was really on the level, I merely laughed nervously. Well, it was Zoltan. That sort of lax, easygoing method was appropriate.

✳   ✳   ✳

My name is Tisse Garland. At present, I'm a steely-eyed hot spring hunter.

It's twilight on the untrod mountain range known as the Wall at the End of the World.

I slipped my body into the water, soaking in the hot springs.

"The temperature is a little on the warm side. A bit too much for children, perhaps, but it would be difficult to come here with kids anyway."

The Wall wasn't a volcanic range, so perhaps the bones of a red dragon lay buried beneath the ground nearby.

Red dragons were a species that no longer existed. The strongest of monsters, they'd once established an empire spanning the world. Legend had it that they were neither good nor evil, and thus during the battle between Demis and the demon overlords, they'd made no attempt to side with either faction. This had led to them being split in half, the split giving rise to the radiant dragons of light and the ash dragons of darkness.

I could not speak to the veracity of that, but it was a documented fact that hot springs and unique kinds of plants appeared in areas where red dragon bones rested beneath the ground.

"I don't know what sort of battle may have occurred out here, but if that is why we are able to enjoy this hot spring now, then may blessings be with the dragon's soul."

While the water felt quite good, it was indeed just a little too hot. Fortunately, stones that were just the right size for someone my height had been placed around the edge of the hot spring. I could maintain a perfect position by sitting on one—my upper body was exposed to the cold air while my lower half was submerged. I smiled comfortably as the mountain breeze blew.

"Truly superb. High marks indeed. And this view…"

The sunset bathed the sky, ground, and sea in red. Night's approach was clear to see. It was a breathtaking sight.

"Ninety-five points. The only issue is the distance from Zoltan."

It was a four-day hike out along a mountain path inhabited by monsters far stronger than those near Zoltan. It was so secluded that even I was considering coming only once every six months.

"Such a shame."

Yet in the moment, it was undeniably a perfect one-hundred-point hot spring experience. I was brimming with satisfaction, totally content with the bath.

"Maybe I should bump it to once every five months…"

"Tisse," Ruti called out to me. Turning my attention away from the vista, I saw Ruti and Yarandrala approaching me through the water. Rit seemed to be calling for Red to come over. He was typically not shy about flirting with her, but he possessed an oddly strong sense of virtue when it came to certain things, so he likely wouldn't approach.

"Tisse," Ruti said again.

"Ah, sorry. What is it?"

"I heard that you and Yarandrala fought."

"Ah…umm, it was just an unfortunate situation beyond our control. I'm sorry for having pointed a weapon at your comrade, Ms. Ruti."

Ignorant of Yarandrala's relationship with Ruti, I had been fully intent on stopping the high elf, even if it cost me an arm. Who knows what would have happened if Mistorm hadn't helped?

"It's not that." Ruti shook her head. Then she tugged Yarandrala's arm. The high elf woman moved right in front me, standing there with a serious expression.

"Umm…yes?" I asked.

"Ruti told me more about you…so I'd like to say something again."

And then one of the Hero's comrades, one who had saved countless people, lowered her head to me apologetically.

"I learned just how precious you are to Ruti. My attempts to hurt you were wrong, and I'm truly sorry."

"I-it's okay. Besides, in the end neither of us was injured."

"I also learned just how much Zoltan matters to Red and Rit. My attempting to destroy it was as good as seeking to wound them," Yarandrala continued without looking up. "If you hadn't stopped me, I would have done something unforgivable. I am truly grateful to you. Thank you, Tisse."

"The residents have forgotten all about it, so it's fine."

Yarandrala was genuinely atoning and offering her gratitude. I understood that was important, but...we were in a hot spring and she was naked. Her large chest and narrow waist, the curve of her hips, and her smooth thighs... Yarandrala's sculpted high elf body was posed before me like a work of art. She did not attempt to conceal anything.

Having made a living as a hired killer, I was used to being hated, but apologies and gratitude were new. That was why, well, even if I had been used to such things, I probably still would have been at a loss as to how to respond.

"I understand. I will gladly accept both your remorse and your appreciation. So, please, raise your head."

"Thank you." Yarandrala smiled in relief as she looked up.

She indeed was the sort of person Red and the others would put their faith in.

After that, we enjoyed the hot spring and chatted about the adventures Ruti and I had experienced after Yarandrala left the party.

Chapter 5

- - - - - - - - - -

The Gem Giants and the Gem Beast

When morning arrived, Tisse and Godwin started back down while we continued up the mountain. There weren't even animal trails left to follow as we hiked across bare rock and through the underbrush.

Five days had passed since we left Zoltan. When we looked up, the snowy summit was visible. The snowcap sparkled beautifully in the sunlight. The urge to continue to the summit started welling up inside me, but that wasn't our plan, and we hadn't prepared to do it, either.

"Appearing out of nowhere and demanding to join our group. This is why no one likes elves. Buncha blackguards the lot of you," grumbled Mogrim.

"Pardon me? I've been Red's companion since long before you met him, so wouldn't that make you the one who joined after?" Yarandrala shot back.

"That's not what I'm talkin' about! We planned this trip for the four of us! Mistorm at least came ready to hike up in the mountains, but you don't even have the proper clothes for cold weather."

"There was nothing to be done about that, since I was in a hurry. And besides, Red was prepared with spare gear, so it isn't a problem."

"This is the issue with you elves!"

"Plans should be properly arranged, but one mustn't merely be bound by a plan. That's the elven way."

Mogrim and Yarandrala had been at it like that the whole time. I had heard dwarves and high elves didn't get along well, but I wouldn't have anticipated it to be so stereotypically bad.

"I heard you last night, too! Yer tryin' to take Red and them away with you to Kiramin, aren't you?"

"That's on hold for the moment, contingent on what their life is like in Zoltan."

"That! That arrogance! It's a bad habit all your kind share. Out here in Zoltan is way better than living surrounded by swarms of snooty elves."

"The biased attitude of this dwarf reflects poorly on Zoltan."

When Yarandrala had first found us yesterday, she and Mogrim had kept a tense distance, but once each understood there wasn't a deep-seated animosity, they started bickering.

"My mental image of Yarandrala has definitely changed," Rit commented with a wry smile.

"Despite how it might seem, she actually has a pretty playful personality," I replied.

It was difficult to sum up Yarandrala in just a few words. At times, she set the group's mood and raised everyone's spirits, but she could also be the reliable, wise one who supported her more reckless companions. Yet there were occasions when she conducted herself like a capricious cat, free and selfish. She was perfectly able to remain indifferent when showered with abuse, but turn that negativity on her companions, and she would get passionately, violently enraged. As the current situation demonstrated, she was also prone to childish arguments.

"But don't let that fool you. Yarandrala's a good person, and totally dependable. She's a true friend," I assured Rit.

She nodded. "Yeah, I trust her."

"Right, after the battle with the demon lord's army, you were on pretty good terms with her, weren't you? With her personality, she doesn't really let too many people get that close."

"Heh-heh. That's because we share a common interest we could talk about."

"Oh? You and Yarandrala? I wonder what that is."

Rit fixed her gaze on me as I pondered.

"I expect I'll have a nice, loooong talk with her about it when we get back."

"R-really?"

I tilted my head, puzzled. Rit seemed to have a bounce in her step.

*   *   *

The gem giant village was near the entrance to the jewel mine they had created. All giants absorbed energy from their environment to maintain themselves in place of relying solely on the food they consumed. Upper-tier species of giants rivaled dragons in strength and possessed more developed societies than they. What limited their sphere of influence was that they grew weaker when they left the environment they had been born in.

In the gem giants' case, they gained nourishment by cutting and processing jewels. To them, mining and cutting gems was a necessity for survival.

"We didn't come to fight. We've come to see about negotiating a deal."

I raised my hands, showing I wasn't holding a weapon to express that I bore no ill will.

When our group approached the entrance of the mine, three gem giants surrounded us. Each was about three and a half meters tall. Their bodies were boulder-like masses of muscle with bands of coloration, and they had thick, bushy eyebrows and smooth, round jaws. Structurally, they vaguely resembled humans, though with some significant differences. Mole-like claws sprouted from their hands, which the gem giants used to burrow through bedrock and cut jewels. Each had eyes of a single solid color, not unlike gems themselves. Growing from their shoulders were small, winglike crystals. That was apparently where gem giants stored their energy. Those crystals could be processed like precious stones, so many adventurers hunted gem giants.

However, the creatures were mid-tier giants and not to be under-estimated. Most everyone knew stories of them destroying towns after adventurers evoked their wrath.

"Turn back. We have no business with you," one of the gem giants commanded, brandishing its claws at us in a warning.

Looks like they are on guard.

"As you can see, we've come with glass prepared. Could you not accept us into your village as guests?" I requested.

The giants exchanged whispers as I held out the marbles. They were clearly excited. Glass was certainly valuable to gem giants, but I hadn't ever received such an excited reaction before. Maybe that was just because manufactured items hardly ever made it out to such a remote location.

"...Come...," one of the giants entreated.

"Hey, doesn't this feel a little off?" Yarandrala whispered.

"Indeed. It seems almost like they've been driven into a corner by something," Mogrim responded quietly.

The two weren't wrong. The way the gem giants were looking at us wasn't normal.

They led us into the gem mine they had dug out with their bare hands. Right when I glanced back to ask Mistorm for a light spell, I sensed an intense menace from behind. I reflexively dodged out of the way, and the next instant, a gem giant's foot stomped down right where I had been standing. I moved in and knocked the creature's legs out from under it, breaking its balance and sending it crashing to the floor. The other two swiped at me with their claws.

"Gragh?!"

A small burst of flame scorched their bodies, and they were forced to pat it out frantically.

"M-magic?! But they didn't form any seals?!"

The giants panicked because they couldn't understand what had happened. And by the time they regained their senses, Rit and Ruti had their swords pressed against the creatures' necks.

"Reserve magic?" I remarked.

It was Mistorm who'd cast the spell. Reserve magic was a technique that those with higher-tier mage blessings could use. By maintaining a powerful spell right on the verge of activation, you could use surplus energy to fire off simple attack spells. In exchange for not requiring a seal, this method couldn't conjure anything beyond simple energy bolts, and until you actually used the powerful magic you were holding in your mind, performing other complex spells was impossible. Still, it was excellent for quick situations.

"Without tricks like that, my magic power wouldn't be much help," Mistorm answered with a chuckle.

Reserve magic wasn't an actual skill; it was born of practice. Learning to use it required talent and long years of diligent study. This was the first time I had ever seen it employed. The old frontier Archmage who had protected Zoltan for decades possessed abilities worthy of a hero.

"Stop, you fools!" sounded an irate shout.

A brawny gem giant considerably larger than the other three emerged from the dark.

I drew my sword, believing it was yelling at us, but its jewellike eyes were focused on its kin. The trio that had attacked us looked ashamed and laid their arms out on the ground as they prostrated themselves before this new giant.

"May I take that to mean you don't intend to fight?"

At my question, the mighty-looking gem giant sat cross-legged on the ground, placed its fists on the surface of the tunnel, and lowered its head until its brow touched the ground.

"Hail, humans, high elf, and dwarf. We have committed a grievous offense, and I humbly beg your pardon."

The enormous creature that easily stood three times taller than us was bowing its head in apology. Rit and I glanced at each other in shock. Neither of us had seen anything like it before.

*   *   *

A mix of merit and seniority decided status among giants. Their system was to count the number of battles that one had participated in and survived. Dishonorable giants that fled to survive were punished and put into indentured servitude, but those that stayed and fought to the end with their comrades had their battles tallied regardless of how many enemies they'd defeated personally.

With that method, leadership would tend to fall to a more prudent, experienced giant rather than a young, hot-blooded one who just happened to be particularly strong. And if the leader's strength failed and it reached a point where it would avoid combat, a new giant would take its place.

"I'm ashamed to say we can't offer anything to make you welcome, but please make yourselves comfortable."

The sturdy gem giant that had apologized to us was one with many fights under its belt and the leader of this tribe. We were sitting across from the chief on owlbear pelts that had been laid on the bedrock for us. Stone cups filled with clear water were given to us all.

"You have our thanks for your kind consideration," I said before draining my cup. Its contents were quite cool, water from an underground spring, maybe?

"Red," Rit whispered concernedly.

I was sure she was wary of swallowing anything provided by a group that had been hostile moments ago.

"It's fine," I assured her.

The gem giants had been holding back, never intending to kill us. Had they been serious, the first one to strike at me would have used his claws, not his foot.

The more time we spent here, the more evident it became that something unusual was occurring. Every gem giant I saw looked exhausted, and they were all just standing there without moving much. There were bones littered all around the floor, proof that they had been eating a lot. But just consuming was not enough for their kind to maintain their enormous forms. That was why most species of giants associated eating with pleasure or thought of it as a pastime.

Excluding particularly slothful varieties like hill giants, traces of past meals lying around was a rare sight in a giant enclave.

"We came to trade this glass for some of your gems," I explained.

The chief looked remorseful. "I'm sorry, but..."

"Please, take the glass first. You can keep it, even if we don't get anything in exchange," I urged.

The listless gem giants around us stirred at that.

"P-please wait," the chief said to its kin before addressing us. "Gems have been scarce of late, and we cannot in good faith accept your offering without trading something of equal value in return."

One of those types with a rigid sense of duty, huh?

"At this rate, won't your people starve? What's keeping you from mining?" I asked.

"So you've already deduced our problem," the chief stated.

"Only the trouble with digging. That much was apparent from looking around. I can't guess the cause."

I took out every marble from the bag and lined them up in front of us.

"If you're unable to pay a fair price, then please just accept these as a gift."

"But—"

"People are starving before our eyes. The adventurer's way is to help those in need."

"...Very well. You have my tribe's gratitude both for your magnanimous tolerance of our indecorous treatment and for bestowing upon us such a blessing in this desperate time. O, human, high elf, and dwarf friends, I swear our tribe shall hold you in the highest friendship for as long as we remain."

Swearing such a heavy oath over this felt a tad extreme.

Given the situation, the glass was as precious to the gem giants as water in a desert, but one bag only cost two quarter payrils. You could buy ten bags with the money it would take to purchase a single cheap obsidian accessory. Swearing all of the tribe's future generations to friendly relations over marbles was a bit much. But proud as the giants were, they likely wouldn't have accepted the glass without that.

"I look forward to a long and fruitful friendship."

I held out my hand, and the giant chief knelt on both knees and reverently took it in both of its own.

✳   ✳   ✳

Altogether there were thirty gem giants in this village. Fortunately, that meant there were enough marbles for each of them, and they wasted no time dexterously cutting the glass with their claws.

"Why?" Ruti asked softly.

"Why what?" I inquired back.

"Why did Demis give them this sort of nature?"

"You mean deriving energy by cutting gems?"

"Yeah. The other giants, too. Iron giants and copper giants refine high-quality metal. Flame giants gain nourishment by destroying civilizations with fire. And yet there are frost giants and sea giants that can subsist purely by existing in an environment suited to them."

The gem giants were processing the glass happily, ravenously... probably like a human would eat a big, juicy steak when they were starving. From a nongiant point of view, it was an odd, illogical scene.

"God created this world. Every living being was crafted with a purpose, just like blessings. Giants are no different in that regard. Thus Demis must have had some reason for granting them this nature, right?" said Ruti.

"I imagine so," I replied.

"...What do you think that purpose was, Big Brother?"

"Presumably the same thing you're thinking—to give other species a reason to fight gem giants."

Why had God created monsters that attacked humans? According to the church's teachings, it gave humans an enemy to combat, that their blessings might develop further. If that really was the case, then the gem giants' nature was undoubtedly derived from the same intent. Besting such a mighty opponent netted you a trove of jewels.

"Mom! Look at what I made!" a young giant shouted.

A female giant looked down at the child's hands and then laughed out loud as it rubbed its kid's head playfully.

Seeing that, Ruti smiled. "Monsters and humans have different values. Negotiations went well this time, but it's more common for them to fail. Fighting may be unavoidable at times, but I would like to believe that monsters exist to be more than just fodder for blessings."

"Me too," I added.

If a religious official heard the Hero say as much, it would cause an uproar. However, if something like the church could stop Ruti, the demon lord's forces wouldn't have fallen before her at every turn. The only thing that had ever fettered my sister was the Divine Blessing of the Hero, and that was no longer an issue.

I was pleased that she had found her freedom as I nodded in agreement with her sentiment.

✳   ✳   ✳

Two hours later, the gem giant chief returned to where we were waiting.

"My apologies for the delay."

The chief's skin was smoother and tauter than before. Its body was overflowing with vitality.

"It's been a long time since we've been able to cut our fill. You have my heartfelt gratitude."

"I'm glad it suited your palate," I replied.

"Indeed. Glass has a bit of an odd flavor, so it can be tiresome in large amounts, but on an empty stomach, glass is as good as diamond."

"I, uh, I see."

I had no idea what sorts of flavors the energy of gemstones could have. Seeing me struggling to respond, Yarandrala started giggling.

"It seems you've recovered enough to be able to joke," she remarked, stepping forward.

Huh? A joke?

The chieftain broke out in a laugh. "Sorry, sorry. It really has been a long time since I've felt like this."

"You seem much improved," I said.

"Indeed."

I guess the chieftain usually kept a decent sense of humor. It was nothing but smiles now.

"So what could have happened for a gem giant village to run out of jewels? Did you exhaust the vein here?" I questioned.

"No, it isn't that. A fell beast that consumes gems has settled into the mine."

A creature that consumed precious stones? And a fell beast, not a monster or a demon. The term evoked a terrifying, dangerous being whose true nature was unknown.

"It eats jewels? And so many that gem giants like yourselves can't even mine any? How many are there?" I questioned.

"Just the one."

"A single beast devouring everything in the mountains?"

"Not only that, it's so powerful that even if all gem giants and other monsters on the peak joined forces, we would still be slaughtered."

"Even an alliance of all the monsters out here isn't enough?"

"I was born and raised on this mountain, so I can't speak for other places…but for us, it would be that one-sided. All of our tribe's warriors have already fallen."

Hmmm.

I had intended this to be a sort of easygoing adventure. Yet a mysterious troublemaker had been lying in wait for us.

*   *   *

Rit and I were out front, Yarandrala, Mogrim, and Mistorm stood in the center, and Ruti acted as the rear guard as we proceeded down into the mine that the gem giants had excavated.

"A monster that can transform nearby gemstones and ore into lead just by its mere presence, huh?" Rit muttered.

The giants had explained as much to us before we left to seek the source of their recent troubles.

"I've never heard of anything like that."

"An unknown monster…"

Of course, there were still many undocumented creatures, particularly in less explored regions like the Wall at the End of the World.

"Still, we can't just leave it be," Mistorm declared. "If we don't deal with it now, it will become a poison to Zoltan."

According to Yarandrala, the presence of this fell beast was what had been weakening the zoogs' forest. Its ability to change ore into lead was contaminating the groundwater and weakening trees.

"The landslide was triggered by the earth growing weaker from that transformation, too," explained the high elf.

Mogrim nodded. "And the rock trolls using lead clubs was due to the lack of iron."

"Perhaps that's why the horses we rode grew so frightened," Mistorm speculated aloud.

This thing had caused practically all the problems we had encountered on this trip.

"We need to defeat it before the lead poisoning spreads to settlements east of Zoltan or to Zoltan's river," I said.

"Are you sure you're okay with this?" Mistorm asked. "I'm the former mayor. Even if I'm retired now, I still bear some responsibility to protect Zoltan. My taking responsibility is why I can get away with a bit of throwing my weight around here and there. But you're different, right? You can't get your gems anymore, and the enemy is a complete mystery that we have no idea how to handle. There's no reason for you to risk your life."

"Even so, I don't think that's reason enough to make you go alone,"

I responded. "Mages can best wield their strength when working in a party. That's one of the first things you learn as an adventurer, right?"

Mistorm's brow furrowed. "Still, we're walking in blindly. There's no guaranteeing your safety."

"This whole world is filled with fighting," Rit said with a grin. "There wasn't ever any guarantee of safety to begin with. And while I may have retired from adventuring, I don't see a reason not to protect Zoltan."

Ruti nodded. "I'm a B-rank adventurer here in Zoltan. I'm used to fighting for someone else's sake...and I've finally gotten to where I can accept doing it once in a while."

Yarandrala checked the seeds that she used for generating plants. "I need to determine whether Zoltan truly is a satisfactory place for my friends to live. Monsters disturbing the peace keeps me from making a fair judgment."

Mogrim glowered at Yarandrala. "This is the problem with high elves. The companions you're traveling with need help, and you require some bigger reason than that?!"

"Unlike dwarves, high elves don't need to enumerate such obvious reasons," Yarandrala fired back peevishly.

"Who's gonna know if you don't say it? This is why people don't trust your kind."

I did my best to calm things down and turned back to Mistorm.

"Anyway, you don't need to worry about us. We're joining this fight because we want to."

"...Sheesh, what a brash and reckless bunch. Thank you."

Zoltan was our home, after all.

*   *   *

There was nothing alive in the mines: no bats, insects, or even moss.

"Red, I can't hear the voices of spirits in here... I won't be able to use my magic," Rit said gravely. Her Spirit Scout blessing drew strength from spirits to enable her to cast spells. In a place absent of them, her magic was inert.

Yarandrala placed her hand on the wall and shook her head. "I can't sense plants, either."

"Does that mean your spells won't work, either?" I asked.

"I can produce vegetation, but not any of my other magic."

"No summoning great spirits, then," I remarked. "We'll have to rely on you for healing, Ruti."

"Leave it to me. There are no issues with my magic or my sword."

"In the end, steel's the great decider, not some elven witchery."

Ruti and Mogrim both looked a little smug.

"What about you, Mistorm...?" I inquired.

"I won't have any problems using my magic. But inside a mine, I can't employ anything too flashy," she explained.

"Looks like we'll have to finish it off at close range, then," I replied.

However, we were up against an opponent that gem giants—which specialized in close-quarters fighting—couldn't beat. It must have some powerful defenses.

"Still, our attack strength has to be higher than theirs, right?" Mistorm questioned.

"Well, yeah," I answered.

Ruti was the strongest person in the world, and Rit and I were two of the greatest sword fighters. Even without her spirit magic, Yarandrala was strong enough to fight a dragon, and Mistorm was an Archmage and an adventurer with decades of experience. And while Mogrim's power was lesser, he could battle on the same level as a gem giant. A party as strong as ours was a rare sight indeed.

"Don't worry, no matter what enemy we face, I'll never lose as long as you're with me, Big Brother," Ruti stated with a glance in my direction.

Smiling, I answered, "Yeah, that's right."

I couldn't shake a vague sense of unease in the back of my mind, however. It almost felt like we were heading to combat an enemy on the level of one of the four heavenly kings of the demon lord's army.

We continued through the caverns, the lantern I held illuminating a path devoid of all life.

And then the fell beast came into view.

$$* \qquad * \qquad *$$

A tunnel dug by giants was wide enough for humans to walk through comfortably. However, the size of this cave was on an entirely different level. It was spacious enough to house Loggervia's castle. The glow of my lantern didn't reach the ceiling. Darkness encircled us as we advanced.

"It's so big...," I muttered.

In the gloom was an enormous shadow, massive enough to make this castle-size chamber feel cramped. The thing's gleaming eyes were as large as I was, and the head they adorned could probably swallow a giant whole. It was almost like a dragon...but there were no wings on its back.

"A turtle?" Ruti tilted her head quizzically.

The beast was titanic, and its shell was studded with countless jewels. Ruti was right, though; it did resemble a turtle.

"I've never seen a monster like this," Ruti admitted.

"Me neither. I fought many creatures in Loggervia, but this is the first I've laid eyes on a turtle so large," Rit responded.

"In all my years, this is an entirely new sight to me," Yarandrala added.

"It's safe to assume this is the thing that's eating the gems, right?" asked Rit.

"Probably," answered Yarandrala with a glance.

"Still, it's a bit disappointing that the fell beast turned out to be a turtle," Mogrim said with a huff.

Mistorm narrowed her eyes. "It should have noticed us by now, but there's still no indication of it attacking."

No.

"It feels like it's just not sure whether to ignore the little bugs flying around it or swat them down," I stated.

"Bugs? What are you talking about?" questioned Mogrim.

"As far as it's concerned, humans, high elves, dwarves—we're all just insects. That thing doesn't have an official name, but some refer to it as a gem beast, because of its appearance."

Rit turned to me. "You know what it is, Red?"

"Only from written accounts. Every record of it is ancient, so I had assumed the story had been embellished. I never suspected a monster like this genuinely existed."

My data on the gem beast hailed from the era of the wood elves. A record of one such creature had been left behind by the warrior who had led a clan called the Irukwa, who had fought alongside the wood elves.

According to that account, the gem beast was responsible for the destruction of the wood elves' forest. In order to save their home, they had gathered human mercenaries and high elves in order to slay the gem beast.

The Irukwa had been among those who'd joined the wood elves, and if their warrior's description was to be believed, the army ran into the horizon.

Mogrim whistled. "So then how'd those warriors defeat a monster like this?"

"They didn't," I answered.

"What?"

"All of the wood elves in the battle died, and only a handful of Irukwa managed to escape. That's all I know about the gem beast."

"No one has ever defeated that thing?"

"Nope."

Even demon lords had fallen to the Hero, but nothing in history suggested someone had slain a gem beast. However, a gem beast had never fought the Hero before.

"Rrrrrr."

The great turtle looked stout, but its cry was clear. When it opened its huge mouth, a horrid stench filled the air and an intense chill went down my spine.

"Something's coming!" I shouted.

The next instant, a bright, white ray erupted from its maw.

"It's okay. Sacred Magic Shield." Ruti stepped in front of us and formed a seal with her left hand. The gleaming barrier of light deflected the gem beast's attack.

"That's—?!" I exclaimed. The wall the beam had struck was covered in sparkling diamonds. "A diamond ray? No, it actually turned the wall's surface into diamonds?!"

An attack that transformed whatever it hit into precious stones. Undoubtedly living things were not excluded from that power.

"…This isn't good…" Ruti arched her eyebrows, looking a little concerned. Cracks were forming in her spell. "It's breaking."

"Wait, your Sacred Magic Shield is shattering?!" I cried in disbelief.

Magic that had withstood even Ares's spells was crumbling before my very eyes. Just as I was about to grab everyone and dash away…

"Thorn Bind!"

…Yarandrala created dozens of thorny vines that constricted the gem beast.

With its mouth bound shut, the force of the attack exploded inside the massive creature's throat and blood started flowing from its ears and eyes.

"Oooh! Not bad for an elf!" Mogrim was genuinely impressed that she had dealt real damage to such an enormous monster.

"Kh…"

However, Yarandrala looked pained and dropped to a knee without responding. The briars she had created turned brown and withered. The gem beast raised its right foreleg to stomp on Yarandrala in retaliation.

"Rit!" I cried.

"Got it!"

Rit leaped out, her shotels slicing into the beast's raised limb. It reflexively drew back from the pain. Its big eyes fell to Rit as it loosed a screeching howl.

"Hiyaahhh!"

Ruti brought an attack down on the gem beast's left foreleg while it was distracted. As it had been supporting itself with that limb, it crashed to the ground.

"I can't put as much power into it as Ruti, but..." I readied my sword beneath where the gem beast's head was falling, staring up at the giant target overhead. Timing my swing against the creature's fall, I combined my own strength with the force of its descent. My blade penetrated its tough skin, ripping through and severing a blood vessel in its neck.

Every monster had a few vulnerable points on its body. That was just the nature of living things. A tiny razor could prove fatal to a human if it cut open an artery in the neck.

There was a jangle as something exploded out of the gem beast's wound.

"J-jewels?" I said with incredulity.

Vibrant gems of all colors were spilling from the gash. I suddenly wasn't so sure that it really was a living creature.

"Oops."

I dashed away from beneath the gem beast's head with my Lightning Speed before it could crush me.

"That's my Red!" Rit praised me.

"It was only because of all of your support! It felt like I landed a clean hit."

Mogrim pointed at the gem beast. "H-hey! It's recovering!"

The wounds Ruti and I had inflicted were mending before our eyes.

"Ah, ghh...!" Yarandrala collapsed with a muffled cry.

"Mrgh." Ruti seemed similarly weakened, her face pained.

Was that why Ruti's and Yarandrala's spells were broken? Had the creature absorbed the magic power they were composed of? I'd never heard of stealing energy from the casters themselves.

"Are you okay, Yarandrala?!" I called.

"I—I think so."

She had run dry on magic power and was undoubtedly suffering extreme fatigue. Her face looked deathly pale.

I looked to my sister. "Ruti?!"

"Enduring things is a specialty of mine."

She had to be feeling the same weakness that Yarandrala was, but she only looked a little annoyed as she readied her sword.

"Red! The jewels!" Rit shouted.

I glanced around and saw that all the diamonds created by the gem beast's attacks were dimming and transforming into lead.

"It's eating the gems it made? That's awfully convenient!" I exclaimed. The diamonds were fueling its recovery. In no time at all, the creature looked good as new. "Now I understand! I had wondered why there weren't any corpses from the gem giants and other monsters who fought it!"

It didn't just consume the ore and gems in the earth; it also used that ray to transform living creatures into jewels and eat them, transforming the diamond into lead.

"The standard tactic for huge things like this is to draw blood from vital points to weaken it. However, magic doesn't work and it can recover with the gems made from its own attack. A typical strategy won't work!" Rit cried as she readied her sword.

She was right. This was a more dangerous enemy than any I had fought before.

"Rrrr."

The gem beast's body shuddered as it moved toward where Yarandrala had collapsed, the ground quaking with each step. Its mere steps alone seemed heavy enough to trample the hardiest warrior.

"Stop it!"

"Right!"

Rit and I charged the monster again. It glanced over at us. Its huge black eyes gleamed red.

"Wh—?!"

Vines sprung up around us.

"Yarandrala's Thorn Bind!"

The spell caught us off guard. We weren't able to dodge it and got entangled.

Ruti leaped over our heads with her sword raised. "I'll—"

Clang!

There was a loud crash. Ruti's attack was stopped in midair.

"My Sacred Magic Shield...!"

A barrier of light had caught my sister's blow. The strongest human's protection magic had blocked her own strike.

"Not good!"

All three of our attacks had been stymied, and the gem beast was not stopping.

"R-run away!" Yarandrala struggled to shout, urging Mistorm and Mogrim to escape. She tried to stand up but couldn't muster the strength and was moving too slowly.

She's not going to make it in time!

"Rrrr?!" the gem beast suddenly howled in agony. An arrow of ice was blooming from its right eye.

"So if I use reserve magic, only the higher-tier magic being held back gets absorbed. I guess that makes sense since I'm not providing the magic power directly... A couple ice arrows for a single high-tier spell is hardly a fair exchange, but you can't make an omelet without breaking a few eggs!"

"This gem beast isn't so different from a drake! Smashing an ax into something'll generally solve the problem!"

Mistorm was holding up her walking stick while Mogrim stood before her, the vanguard to her rearguard caster. An elderly mage and dwarf didn't look too formidable when facing off against a beast the size of a castle, however.

The damage Mistorm had caused was swiftly undone, and the gem beast continued its march, but the two of them did not run.

"Who the hell'd run from such a sweet setup?" said Mogrim.

"A powerful foe before and a fallen comrade behind. When would an adventurer ever show their stuff if not now?" remarked Mistorm before unleashing several ice arrows to curb the gem beast's advance. Stopping such a large monster with a few projectiles was going to be difficult, however. "Eyes, nose, ears, mouth...none of them are enough, huh?"

Even against this overwhelming foe, Mistorm responded like a consummate veteran, accurately hitting every weak spot she could with her low-powered magic. Yet while the gem beast flinched from the blows, every injury quickly mended itself.

"Dorrrryaaaa!" Mogrim roared as he hurled his ax with both hands. There was a whistling sound as it cut through the air and slammed between the gem beast's eyes.

Clang!

The weapon bounced off. The gem beast tilted its head slightly but showed no sign of having been hurt by the impact.

"Hrm. That woulda been enough for something like a rock troll," Mogrim muttered in disappointment as he reached for the spear at his back.

"Please...you have no hope of winning, so just run," pleaded Yarandrala.

"Hmph. You've been too strong for too long, high elf," Mogrim remarked with a sniff.

"What are you saying...?"

"Ordinary people have their own way of fighting, too!"

As the dwarf made his declaration, Rit and I sprinted up the gem beast's legs.

"Thanks, Mogrim!" I said. His ax had rebounded and torn through the vines binding us. "It shouldn't be able to summon Thorn Bind against something so close to it!"

Rit sliced into the back of the massive creature's head with her shotels. "Tough...but I can keep going!" She tenaciously slashed the same place over and over, and before long, the gem beast couldn't take it, pausing its advance to try shaking Rit off.

"There!" I swung my sword down against the gem beast's neck. "Without martial arts or magic, I had to develop several tricks for dealing with monsters like this one where common skills couldn't cut it."

My using the gem beast's weight to cut its neck before had been one such example, and this was another—an attack that sent a shock wave through armor and skin into the opponent's innards.

The beast let out a screech like something shattering, finally stopping. I could feel blood vessels inside its skin rupturing.

Its regenerative abilities far outstripped my attack power. No matter what I did, I wouldn't be able to defeat it with my strength. Yet if its nervous system was damaged, it would pass out like any other living creature. Even if that damage was healed, it would still take time for the gem beast to regain consciousness. It might only be for a short moment, but the creature came to a halt and dropped to the ground.

"Big Brother, can I use all of my power?"

And just like I'd hoped, the Sacred Magic Shield blocking Ruti vanished when the monster lost consciousness.

"Yeah, even if they see you, I'm sure it will be fine. Go wild."

"Okay."

Ruti was always holding back for fear of being revealed as the Hero and having her slow life come to an end. Not that she wasn't already superhuman even when restraining herself, but that was her attempt to keep herself within the realm of a regular adventurer.

There was no sword in her hand. She just clenched her fist as she leaped over the gem beast's head.

"Sacred Magic Shield."

She summoned a barrier of light above her in the air, not for protection but to kick off. And when she did, Ruti rocketed toward the gem beast as surely as any arrow.

"Haaaaaaaaaah!!!!"

Her fist slammed into the creature's head, sending out a thundering shock wave.

The gem beast's corpse collapsed to the ground as a river of gems flowed from the gaping wound where its head had been. A tremor shook the earth, and a crater formed as the bedrock shattered from the force of Ruti landing.

"That's… Heh, nothing to do but be amazed, I guess. What do they make adventurers of nowadays?" Mistorm commented.

A small girl had punched a giant, castle-size monster into the ground.

The gem beast was limp in the crater, its neck sticking out over the side. A small mountain of gems was quickly building behind Ruti.

"Did we do it?!" Mogrim approached cautiously, his spear still in hand.

Meanwhile, Rit and I climbed down from atop the gem beast with our swords still drawn.

"What do you think?" Rit asked.

"I don't know. Hydras can recover after the loss of a head, but there's not enough information about gem beasts to say," I replied.

The massive thing certainly appeared slain.

"It's dead, isn't it? Ooooh!" Mogrim finally reached Ruti's side, his eyes drawn to the river of jewels. "Look at this, Red! Mistorm! It's earth crystal! I've never seen one this big!" The dwarf looked like he might start dancing for joy as he held up a dusky yellow gem the size of a fist. With that much, he could make a knife and have plenty of earth crystal left over.

"Is this one of those all's-well-that-ends-well sort of things?" Rit questioned as she watched him.

"I guess so. And with that many precious stones, we can probably find the blue sapphire I'm looking for, too. And that's probably enough for the gem giant village to live off for the next ten years."

"A happy ending for all," Rit said as we grinned at each other.

"Wait," Yarandrala called out weakly.

"It's okay, Yarandrala. You and Mistorm should pull back for a bit. The gem beast consumed your magic power, so it will take some time for you to recover."

"No…"

"Huh? What is it?"

There was a thud, then a whoosh of something slipping past us and rushing toward the gem beast.

"Aaaaah!" Mogrim screamed. The earth crystal he had been holding lost its gleam and transformed into dull, gray lead.

"It's still alive?!" I exclaimed.

I started to attack the gem beast again, but...

Bam!!!

A violent tremor shook the ground.

Looking all around, I shouted, "What is it now?!"

"Above us!" Yarandrala cried.

Looking up, I spotted several slivers of light running through the high ceiling.

"What's that?" I wondered aloud. A crashing sound rang out as light tore through the darkness. "That's impossible! Meteo?!"

It was Ares's specialty, an enormous spell that brought a meteor crashing down. Sunlight was pouring in from the gaping hole torn by the meteor. This wasn't an attack to be used in an enclosed space, yet it had barreled through the mountain itself to crash down on us.

"The ceiling's collapsing!" I warned.

With Ruti's or Yarandrala's magic we could defend against it, but the odds were hardly in our favor. At this rate, I was going to have to use my last resort. But before I could take action, Mistorm raised her staff overhead and directed it at the meteorite.

"Guess I'll play the ace up my sleeve!" Magic power surged around the old woman. It was so intense it surpassed the power of a top-tier spell. Whatever she was attempting demanded every ounce of her energy. "Blackened blood, words of annihilation, pierce paradise overlord's spear! The time of destruction has come! Demon's Flare!"

A dark inferno burst forth from Mistorm's staff. The flames slammed into the meteorite, engulfing it in swirling shadow. It and the falling rocks were quickly consumed.

Even Rit couldn't hide her astonishment. "Amazing..."

This was a massive spell the likes of which even an adventurer of

Rit's caliber had never seen before. I had only seen it once before myself.

Why can she use that magic? No, save it for later. With that much power, it should be able to counter Meteo.

Unfortunately...

"Kh. You can even absorb magic power not directed at you...?" Mistorm muttered in disgust.

The ebon blaze swallowing the meteorite was being drawn toward the gem beast. About half of the meteor had been seared away, but it was still powerful enough to destroy this mine. Even knowing it was pointless, Mogrim stood in front of Mistorm with his spear to protect her.

"Is this how it ends?" The despair was starting to show on the dwarf's face.

Ruti could smash the falling rock, but the fragments would still annihilate everything around us. We needed magic for everyone to get out of this intact.

"...I guess there really isn't any other choice...," I muttered.

"Is there something you can do, Red?!" Rit asked frantically.

"Yeah... I don't know what will come of it, but we hardly have a choice now." I steeled my resolve. "Rit, um, sorry."

"Huh?"

I dashed over to Yarandrala with my Lightning Speed. She was gritting her teeth, mortified at her helplessness.

"Yarandrala!"

"Red...!"

I scooped her up in my arms and pressed my lips against hers.

"Mhm?!"

I created a mental image of my own body's warmth and her body's merging just like I had been taught long ago. And then I imagined a flame lighting inside me. The heat of it poured into Yarandrala.

If my body starts feeling colder, that means it's working... There!

"Haah."

A powerful wave of exhaustion hit me as I pulled away from

Yarandrala to keep from getting in her way. However, her arms firmly drew me in.

"The spirits have come in through the hole in the ceiling. This will work!" the high elf declared, her eyes shimmering. "Source of mana, ruler of all things! Great spirit of the mighty tree!"

Countless briars burst from the ground, twining together and forming a giant entity.

As if responding to her mental state, the spirit roared as white petals filled the air.

"Y-Yarandrala! I don't have that much magic power! You don't have to use something so big! Just enough to protect everyone from the meteorite!"

"It's not a problem! This is the strength you gave me!"

The great spirit wrapped countless tendrils around the meteorite.

"*Grooooooooh!*"

Back when we had been adventuring together, Yarandrala had summoned this spirit before, but this was the first time I had ever heard it roar. Mistorm smiled when she saw what was happening.

"I've about reached my limit... I'll leave the rest to you."

Her spell, which had been holding the meteor at bay, vanished. As the mass of fiery rock resumed its descent, the spirit tugged at the tendrils wrapped around it, changing the meteor's course so that it fell on the gem beast instead of us.

"Rrrr?!"

The monster withdrew its head into its jewel-encrusted shell. The meteor collided with it, and another shock wave shook the mine. A deafening crash erupted while dirt filled the air, making it impossible to see.

*   *   *

There was a thud as rubble scattered, and I saw something shining down from above.

The squarish golem holding us set us down on the ground.

We're outside the mines?

Looking around, I saw that we seemed to be above a cliff formed by the mountain's ridge. The clearing was wide enough, but there wasn't a path down, and it was a dizzyingly long drop.

"Thank you," Rit said, patting the golem.

The thing was just a figure sculpted from dirt, so it couldn't have any expression, yet it appeared pleased.

Just like Yarandrala had been able to summon the great spirit once the meteor had punched a hole in the cavern ceiling, Rit had conjured a golem to carry us to safety. Yarandrala's eyes were still closed as she continued to focus on maintaining the tree spirit. Both it and the gem beast were still buried inside the mine.

What's going on down there?

Mogrim placed an ear to the ground. "They're coming!" he shouted.

Two giant figures burst from the opening Meteo had carved, pushing their way through the rubble as they continued their fight. The gem beast's shell had been shattered by the meteor.

Several of the great spirit's tendrils jabbed into the gem beast's body, sapping its vitality, but the monster was absorbing magic power from the spirit in kind. Several of the spirit's vines dried out, limply drifting to the ground. Despite that, the gem beast's miraculous regeneration ability didn't seem to be taking effect. The great spirit evidently had the upper hand.

"Yarandrala, are you okay?" I asked.

"…I-I'm fine…"

Her summoned construct was leeching energy from the gem beast, so Yarandrala's magic depletion wasn't critical yet, but her power was gradually being absorbed because of her link to the spirit. Yarandrala would run out at this rate before the gem beast was defeated, and her conjured warrior would disappear.

"We've got to do something about that draining," I muttered weakly, struggling to deal with the enervation of magic deficiency, which I had never experienced before.

"Big Brother," Ruti called as she looked at her hands. "The gem beast's blessing should be sealed."

"Hmm? You mean with the power of your New Truth?" I asked.

"Yeah. But its movements only got a little slower."

"That—that shouldn't be possible."

Even if the gem beast's ability to sap magic and heal was innate, that it could be so effective without the enhancement of a Divine Blessing was unheard of. What's more, it had cast Meteo after Ruti had punched it and sealed its blessing. It was impossible to use spells without a blessing.

"I think…" Ruti turned her gaze to the gem beast. Its head had fully regenerated, and it was gradually starting to overwhelm the spirit. "I think it has multiple blessings."

My gut reaction was to denounce that as impossible. One life, one Divine Blessing was the fundamental principle of this world that Demis had created. Or at least, it was supposed to be.

However, an exception was already standing right in front of me. Ruti was proof of a being with two blessings. I couldn't declare her claim impossible, so I nodded.

"So then it became that powerful by enhancing a single body with countless blessings?" I wondered.

Blessings like Magic-Sealing Swordsman and Spell Thief were known to exist. While they couldn't steal magic power from a person, if the gem beast was activating multiple magic-absorbing blessings at once, then that could explain it.

Considering this, I reasoned, "The best move might be to lower its blessing level with the wild elf medicine."

I pulled a vial of the substance I had given Ademi to lower his blessing's skill level out of the pouch at my waist. Its intended use was for suppressing the impulses of blessings, so it couldn't lower a blessing level by a substantial amount. Still, if the gem beast achieved its draining effect by activating several skills all at once, the medicine could have an outsize effect. The only issue was…

"How do we get it to take the medicine?"

The gem beast was in the middle of an intense fight with the great spirit, and someone needed to weave through that battle and throw the medicine into the gem beast's mouth.

"I'll do it," Ruti declared as she clenched her fist.

"No, I want you to be able to attack once you've confirmed this idea works. It could be dangerous if it uses poison-neutralizing spells," I replied.

"Understood. But then who will make it swallow?"

"I'll do it. At least, I'd like to, but I'm still a little sluggish from giving Yarandrala my magic power."

Rit's hand shot straight up.

"I can handle it!" She was holding a shotel in her left hand as she held out her right to me. "I'm ambidextrous since my natural style is dual-wielding, so I won't have trouble throwing it while fighting."

"Yeah, you're probably the best choice for this," I agreed.

"Leave it to me!"

"Hey, what are you mumbling about over here?" Mogrim demanded as he clomped back over after having checked on Mistorm. "I dunno what's going on, but if tossing stuff's what you need, then I'm the dwarf for the job, since I've mastered the Throwing skill."

That gave me pause. "Hmm."

When it came to the actual act of throwing, Mogrim was the best of all of us. Rit had taken a skill to use throwing knives and had trained it, but the ability was merely a way of dealing with attacks from long range, where she had fewer options.

"…You take care of Mistorm since she can't move. We'll go with a formation centered around Rit with Yarandrala and me as support," I said to Mogrim. It was clear as day that the dwarf wasn't pleased about this decision, though.

His aim would be truer, and he could probably use his Ricochet Toss to land the medicine in the gem beast's mouth. But Rit and I had teamwork that was not to be underestimated.

I placed the medicine in Rit's hand.

"Your ability to throw is better, Mogrim, but Rit and I share a bond, and that's more reliable than any skill."

"Ugh, I'm amazed you can say something like that with a straight face," Mogrim remarked.

"It's because it's the truth."

The dwarf burst into laughter and then started nodding. "Even at a time like this... Fine, fine, I got it. Just leave the rear to me."

I stood next to Rit and took a deep breath, getting myself ready.

"Okay, I think I can manage. It's not like I'm totally out of magic power, so I can still move."

"I never knew there was a method for sharing magic power without using spells or skills," Rit said.

"Er, yeah, it's a technique passed down by elves."

"I'll be expecting a detailed explanation later."

Rit's smile was terrifying, but I had to focus on the gem beast! I definitely wasn't trying to avoid anything. Not at all.

"Let's go!"

"Yah!"

Rit and I both started running. I stepped out in front first.

"Yarandrala!" I shouted.

A single tendril from the great spirit approached us. I dashed up the thick vine and leaped into the air. While the gem beast and great spirit were locked in an epic struggle, I landed on another tendril that was wrapped around the gem beast's neck.

Noticing me, the turtle-like creature opened its mouth to swallow me whole. I dashed to evade and slashed with my sword.

There was an unpleasant sound of a joint breaking as the gem beast's maw hung limply open. The great spirit's vines pushed into the gem beast's mouth, forcing it wide. The jaw joint was regenerating, but the tendrils were keeping it open.

"Now!"

Rit had been ready to throw even before I said anything. Unfortunately...

"Rrrr!!!"

A bright ray exploded from the gem beast's mouth.

"Rit!"

The ray struck her and the great spirit dead-on. The spirit shuddered as diamonds scattered around it. Rit's coat, now a mass of diamonds, went tumbling to the ground. She had used it as a shield. With her free arm, she hurled the wild elf medicine. Rit's trajectory had changed after she blocked the gem beast's beam, though, and the angle of her throw was off. The medicine was still going to land in the beast's mouth, but it would just hit its upper palate and spread across its tongue.

That was where I came in.

"That's my Rit!!!" I cried, and I immediately jumped up to bat the airborne vial with the flat of my sword, sending it to the back of the gem beast's throat. There was an audible swallowing sound, and the creature appeared stunned for a moment before collapsing like a puppet whose strings had been cut. Its abrupt drop caused a tremor.

"It can't stand on its own without a blessing?" I observed with incredulity.

Can such an illogical creature really exist?

The gem beast awkwardly struggled as it clung to the ground.

"You aren't one of God's creations, are you?" Ruti said as she leaped atop its shell. "The symbols engraved on your shell are ancient elf script. They made you." My sister closed her eyes for a brief moment. "They are the ones in the wrong, but I'm sorry, we can't coexist with you."

Opening her eyes, Ruti drove her fist straight down into the monstrous turtle.

"I battle to protect the place where the people I love reside. The world I can reach with my own two hands. I'm not some hero of justice anymore. This is my life now. I fight because I want to and not because I'm bound by some sense of duty imposed by the Hero."

There was an explosion as the gem beast's enormous body shattered.

Its limp body made no further attempts to restore itself. We had finally dealt a lethal blow.

Yet…

"That's…?!"

Even Ruti was dumbfounded by what came next.

Driven by what had to be an obsession, the gem beast's shredded neck twisted and aimed its head at the high elf who resembled its creators. With the creature's final breath, it loosed a ray at her. It lacked the strength to transform Yarandrala into gems, but the ray was more than enough to send the exhausted woman flying.

Yarandrala's body went soaring through the air toward the cliff. The gem beast's head slammed to the ground and ceased moving, its tongue lolling out of its mouth.

"Grab my hand!"

I sprinted using Lightning Speed and jumped off the cliff. I grabbed Yarandrala's outstretched hand and pulled her close, so we fell together.

*   *   *

"Are you okay?" Yarandrala asked while glancing anxiously at my ankle.

"Yeah, just twisted my foot a bit is all," I responded with a reassuring smile before looking down. "Still, though, that gave me goose bumps."

The wind whistled past us, and the grasslands far, far below us quivered in the breeze.

Yarandrala and I were sitting in a little hollow in the middle of the sheer cliff face. I had used my Slow Fall skill to kick the natural rock wall and slow our descent. Miraculously, we'd managed to land in this alcove.

"It would've all been over if I fell from here, high blessing level or not."

There were another two hundred meters at least to the bottom of the cliff. It was a dizzying height.

"Are you okay, Red?!" Rit shouted from above.

"Yeah! We're safe! We're in a little cave in the cliff face! The wind is strong, so be careful coming down!" I yelled back.

"Got it!"

The gem beast was finally dead. There wasn't any danger left. Ruti, Yarandrala, and Mistorm had used up their magic power, but Rit would be able to reach us with her Levitate.

"All that's left is to relax and wait," I said cheerfully.

Yarandrala was staring out at the view.

"It's lovely."

"Yeah, it sure is."

Clear blue skies and the vibrant green landscape of Zoltan extended into the distance. Far away, white clouds were floating above the sea, gradually drifting toward the river Zoltan was built around, where a herd of wild horses was bathing. Wyverns glided over the plains.

"Zoltan isn't such a bad place," Yarandrala admitted with a smile.

"You finally understand?" I asked.

"I'll give up on taking you back with me to Kiramin for now."

"Ah, so you still haven't totally accepted it."

"High elves are at least as stubborn as dwarves."

"True. For having such opposite personalities, you're pretty similar in some weird ways."

"Hee-hee, but you know, both high elves and dwarves will gladly accept it if you can convince them you are right…and I've started to think you, Rit, and Ruti can find happiness here."

The cave we were sitting in was narrow, enough that our shoulders were touching as we gazed at the beautiful landscape.

"Gideon, are you happy now?" Yarandrala inquired while still looking out.

"Reddddd!"

Rit was gradually floating down toward us using her magic. I waved up at her and could see her beaming.

"Yeah, I'm very happy."

✳   ✳   ✳

Rit held on to Yarandrala and me as we returned to the top of the cliff.

No sooner did we land than Ruti ran over and smothered me in a hug.

"Are you all right, Big Brother?"

She had probably wanted to come get us herself, but with her magic power drained, she had yielded that responsibility to Rit.

"Thanks for worrying about me. I'm fine. As you can see, it's nothing too bad…I just twisted my ankle a bit."

"Mrgh."

Ruti looked at my leg and then back at her own hands before slumping her shoulders, disappointed that she didn't have the power left to heal me.

I gently patted her head.

"I appreciate the thought."

Looking at the corpse of the gem beast, I saw that the monster had become a dull hunk of lead. The diamonds created by its attacks during the fight and all the other gems stored up inside its body had become lead as well.

"Is there no earth crystal?!"

Mogrim scoured the lead for any remaining gems. I would have liked to help, but I had to rest for a bit.

"Haaah, that was a bother. At this age, my body really can't keep up," Mistorm complained as she lay stretched out on the ground. "Still, had I gone alone, I wouldn't have had any hope of winning. I owe you."

Archmage was a blessing that specialized in mystic art spells, so the gem beast's ability to leech magic had made it the worst possible enemy for Mistorm. And the gem beast had rivaled the strength of Desmond of the Earth, one of the demon lord's four heavenly kings, whom I had fought back during my time in the Hero's party. Who knew what would have happened if Ruti hadn't been here?

"Ruti."

"Yes?"

"Thank you for coming with me."

"Was I helpful?"

"Yeah, I don't know what I would have done without you."

"Yay!" My sister smiled happily.

"I'd love for you to come with me on future trips, too, so long as you aren't busy. Having you around is great."

"Mhm! I'll absolutely come with you!"

Ruti happily embraced me.

What an adorable little sister.

I thought I heard my hip pop. That Ruti was so happy that she didn't control her strength entirely was proof of how adorable she was.

I really do have an amazing sibling.

All of a sudden, a loud clatter broke our peaceful moment together. Looking back, I saw Mogrim had fallen backward.

"Are you okay?!" I exclaimed.

"R-Red! C'mere!"

I gently pulled away from Ruti and hurried over.

"What is it?"

"T-take a look at this."

"This is…"

There was a gem about the size of a thumb in Mogrim's hand. It looked red at first, but the shine changed colors as I examined it, turning blue, yellow, and purple, too.

"So there was a gemstone that survived. It doesn't seem like an earth crystal… This is… Wait, is that…"

"Yeah! It's an iridescent ruby! Every smith's dream!"

Mogrim was trembling in excitement, not even bothering to stand back up.

Iridescent rubies were legendary. They were said to have the prop-
erties of every material. It was rumored they could be used to make
weapons and armor harder than diamond, more durable than steel,
capable of cutting through anything and enduring any impact.

The Holy Demon Slayer Ruti had wielded was a sword forged from
iridescent ruby by Demis, if the myths were to be believed. It was a
stone rare enough to have legends about it, and just like Mogrim said,
it was something every smith dreamed of.

"Are you sure?" I questioned.

"How should I know?! It's not like I've ever seen a real iridescent
ruby before. Other than the fabled dwarf kings, no dwarf has. All I
know is this is a gem I've never seen before, and it looks the same as
iridescent rubies are described!" Mogrim leaped to his feet. "There
might be more!"

And with that, he started tearing through the heaps of lead.

"...But I want something that suits Rit a little better...," I muttered,
glancing at all the piles of lead.

No matter where I searched in the heaps of dull gray, I couldn't find
anything with a sky-blue gleam to match Rit's.

Our group took an hour's break to recover somewhat from magic
exhaustion.

After that, we would either go back to the gem giants' village to
report or else walk and rest a bit more. Either way, we would be sleeping early tonight. It had been that exhausting a battle for everyone.
However, Mogrim was still tirelessly searching through the lead piles.
His was a tenacity and mental fortitude befitting a dwarf.

As for the rest of us, Ruti watched the clouds wafting through the
sky, Yarandrala was holding a branch of holly with her eyes closed,
and Mistorm was sitting cross-legged on a mat. All three of them were
concentrating to recover their magic power.

Rit's eyes were locked on me. Her expression was different than usual. "Red."

"Wh-what is it?"

"I would like an explanation for the action you executed to transfer power to Yarandrala," she stated, looking displeased.

"It is a technique passed down among high elves. It doesn't require spells or skills, only physical contact. However, when performed where there is a thinner layer of skin, for example, with both parties connecting across mucous membranes, the efficacy of the transfer increases significantly. Likely the theory behind it is something similar to the draining abilities employed by succubus demons or vampires. From a pure transfer-efficacy perspective, optimal results would be had if both parties opened a cut and maintained contact via the wounds, but that would hurt, be unsanitary, and generally just cause more problems all around. Thus, linking through the lips is the most practical method available, and given the situation, I judged it to be a necessary action," I explained, nervously watching Rit's reaction.

"I understand you had a good reason…ugh…but!" She thumped my chest lightly. "I want to know more of what you know. I want to know everything about you. Compared to Yarandrala, I've been with you for such a short time…"

"Okay, I understand, Rit."

"What? Eh?!"

I kissed her, and just like before, I transferred my magic. Rit's eyes went wide in shock, but she quickly untensed and gazed into my eyes with a drowsy, almost intoxicated stare. When I pulled away, Rit sighed.

"…Now you understand that part of me, too," I declared.

"It's like a warm strength poured into me. It still feels like it's flowing around inside of me," Rit remarked as she squeezed herself. "This… This is a wonderful thing! I could get addicted to this sensation!"

"Ah-ha-ha. I'm glad you liked it… Ghk."

My vision blurred.

"Red?!" Rit frantically shifted to support my wobbling body.

"Passing magic power to someone else is fine and all, but I don't have precise control of the technique. I gave you all of my magic power just now."

"Whaaaat?"

"Ahhh, so this is why Yarandrala and Mistorm can't move. My body isn't responding at all."

Had Rit not been there, my face would have collided with the ground.

Ruti was really fighting while feeling like this? That's amazing.

Rit's face paled. "Red! Are you okay?!"

"It's not life-threatening or anything, but my muscles aren't responding. You can just set me down somewhere."

"On the ground…?"

Rit hugged me close. Maybe my body temperature had fallen from magic exhaustion, but Rit's warmth was comfortable and inviting. Before I realized it, I was growing drowsy.

"Still, this is a bit of a problem. I don't know how to recover magic power like Ruti or the others… I might not be able to move for a while…," I confessed.

"Then just lean on me."

Rit shifted me to a position that wouldn't be uncomfortable and sat down. Now she was hugging me from behind.

"Aren't I heavy?" I asked.

She shook her head. "It's a pleasant weight."

"Really?"

My eyelids were heavy now, and my mind was begging for rest. I was trying to endure, but even my soul was crying out for a break. There was no way to hold on, and I could feel my consciousness slipping away.

"It's fine. You can fall asleep. I'll stay by your side."

"…I… If you…say so… Thanks…"

I don't know how I even managed to reply. I touched Rit's hand, making sure she was there. Reassured, I stopped fighting it.

*   *   *

"You really fell asleep."

Red had passed out with a peaceful look on his face while resting against Rit. The young woman squeezed him, adjusting the unconscious man slightly to be in a more comfortable position.

"Eh-heh-heh."

Rit giggled and then blushed as she looked around.

Mistorm's eyes were closed, but it was clear she was holding back a chuckle, and Ruti was staring straight at Red.

Ruti is always using the excuse of being siblings to cling to him! Is it wrong for me to do it, too? thought Rit.

If Mogrim had been able to hear her thoughts, he would have shot back, "What do you mean? You do that just as much as she does!" But he was absorbed in his search for gems, so even if he'd possessed a mind-reading skill, he would've kept quiet.

And so Rit's mental resolution to be more aggressive about flirting with Red went unnoticed.

She alternately gazed out at the winter sky and peered down at Red's face.

He was sleeping defenselessly in her arms, which made Rit indescribably happy. The breeze was frigid on the mountain, and because she'd thrown away her coat during the fight, her skin was cold, but that just emphasized the contrast with the warmth in her arms. It felt like the love welling up inside her was going to burst.

"Sorry, I didn't mean to upset you."

Rit was absorbed in her feelings, so she twitched in shock at the sudden voice. Yarandrala was smiling as she beheld Rit.

"Don't scare me like that."

"Ah-ha-ha, but I wasn't even particularly trying to sneak up on you."

Rit blushed. They were still out on a dangerous mountain, and she had gotten so absorbed in her moment with Red that all else had faded away.

"I'd like to chat with you a bit if you don't mind," requested Yarandrala.

Rit nodded, and the high elf took a seat next to her.

"How was the magic transfer?"

"'How' as in...?"

"It was a rapturous feeling, right?"

"Y-yeah."

"At the purest level, it's accepting a part of someone you love and making it a part of you. I'm sure the first elf who discovered this technique was a passionate person," Yarandrala remarked.

Rit looked at Red and smiled happily. "Yeah, I agree. I don't think it was developed for combat. It must have originated from something more beautiful than that."

Yarandrala peered over at Red's sleeping face. "He's changed."

"Changed?" Rit asked.

"In a good way. The old him would never have allowed himself to be so defenseless while out on a dangerous mountain. Not only that, he transferred magic to you outside of necessity. The Red I knew would never have done that," Yarandrala said as she gently patted his head. "The first time we met, he was still a knight in training, only nine years old. He was so cute walking around in a child-size knight outfit."

"What? I wish I could have seen that."

"I secretly sketched a portrait back then. I can show you later." Yarandrala's eyes were fixed upon Red's face. "Small as he was, Red was more active than any of the other pages and squires in the capital. He took dangerous mission after dangerous mission, and the days he was off duty, he worked as an adventurer...all to become just a little bit stronger for the day his little sister would eventually set off on her journey."

"He's mentioned it before, but..."

"Of course, it's thanks to that effort that he can act this way now. Still, I always wanted him to find happiness as just Red rather than having to continue fighting as a hero."

"Yarandrala...," Rit muttered.

A lovely smile crossed the high elf's face, like a flower blooming.

"When he was driven out of the party, I thought he must have been suffering. He was always battling, all to be able to help Ruti in her quest, and I couldn't help thinking just how hopeless he must have felt to have that stolen. But I was wrong! You were there for my precious friend!"

"Only because you supported me," Rit added.

Yarandrala raised a questioning eyebrow. "That time in the bewitching woods?"

"Yeah. I had this image of him as perfect, a hero even greater than Ruti. But it was just like you said. There were things he didn't know and things he didn't notice. And that just made me love him even more."

"I'm glad you're the person he fell for."

Overcome with emotion, Yarandrala suddenly kissed Rit. Rit's eyes went wide from shock, and she was a little confused, but then she remembered that high elves expressed deep affection physically.

Even though Yarandrala was used to human society, her nature showed through in charged moments.

After thinking for a little bit, Rit decided, "Yeah, I definitely can't go to Kiramin."

"Really? Kiramin's a nice place, too," Yarandrala replied.

"I'm sure." Rit squeezed the man in her arms tightly before whispering softly, "But Red's lips are mine."

✳   ✳   ✳

When I opened my eyes, the sun was already starting to get low in the sky.

I had only meant to rest for an hour, but evidently, I'd taken far more time. I shot up upon realizing the time, yet everyone smiled and assured me there was no need to rush since the view was so lovely.

While I was out, Rit's golems had been working to clear a passage back into the mines. It was a small opening, but it was enough for people to pass through, and while we got our knees a little dirty crawling, we managed to make it safely back to the gem giants' tunnels.

When we made it back to the village and reported that we had slain the gem beast, the giants were stunned. They were even more awestruck by the iridescent ruby Mogrim showed them as proof of the monster's death.

That night, we enjoyed our second feast of the trip.

"For as long as I've been called Rit the hero, I've never experienced something like this before. Guest at another feast thrown by monsters. A trip like this feels odd after settling into a slow life," Rit said.

"Since we're not in a rush to get somewhere or accomplish a goal, we have the opportunity to experience new and different things, I guess," I answered.

Even to us humans, the portions of food laid out were definitely on the small side.

Gem giants didn't have any knowledge of farming and hadn't developed any techniques for it. Furthermore, there weren't many animals you could hunt up at this altitude. Today's meal was baked wild fowl and vegetables with a sauce made from ground nuts. The food itself was nothing special, but the dishes it was served on were quite remarkable. The giants had apparently made them by processing the glass I had brought. They glittered as surely as any true precious stones.

The food was presented in a precise geometric arrangement on the dishes, creating a presentation worthy of a feast for otherwise average food. Such a display felt appropriate for the dexterous gem giants.

"Fascinating."

Ruti seemed to enjoy sampling giant cooking for the first time ever.

Mogrim wore a long face, and his eyes were cast down while everyone else ate.

Curious, I asked, "What is it, Mogrim?"

"Hmm? Nothing..."

"What, not feeling well?" Mistorm questioned.

"Were you injured?" Yarandrala added.

Mogrim glanced up with a dejected look.

"It's just, we defeated the gem beast, but it had already consumed all the jewels around here, right? I was just wondering what will happen to the gem giants now."

In the end, we had only recovered the one iridescent ruby from the gem beast. Even if we gave it to the giants, that wouldn't be enough to fulfill their energy needs.

"That's nothing a guest needs to be fret over," the gem giant chief responded cheerily. "We can ration the glass you gave us and survive awhile longer. If we can find another vein while that lasts, then there won't be a problem, and if we can't, then that's it. We've been quite blessed as it is. If we aren't able to endure, then that is just fate."

"But"—Mogrim eyed the gem giant family smiling cheerfully behind him and then turned his head down—"I still want to do something…"

Mistorm crossed her arms in thought. I examined a glass bowl filled with food and was suddenly struck by an idea.

"Hey, Rit, Mistorm, Mogrim. How much do you think this glass dish would sell for in Zoltan?"

"Hmm, for something like this, even on the low end, you could get about ten payrils, at least."

"I agree, it is valuable, but are there any traveling merchants who would come all the way out here to buy it? And gem giants coming down to a human village to trade would cause a big fuss, so that's out."

"And if you put in a quest for adventurers, it'd be too expensive to be worth it."

Each reply was fairly sensible.

"What about if it was the zoog village?" I proposed.

"The zoog village? Ahhh…that we could probably manage." Mistorm nodded.

"What are you thinking, Red?" Rit pressed.

Zoogs claimed they couldn't understand commerce, even though they needed meat, because they could not comprehend weighing the values of different things against one another. They struggled to deal with merchants because they didn't know a fair price from an exploitative one.

"If a merchant gives glass to the zoogs, the gem giants can hunt to get meat to trade the zoogs for the glass, and then the gem giants can cut the glass to replenish their energy and leave the cut glass with the zoogs to keep the cycle going," I outlined.

In this way, the dangerous leg of the route between the zoog village and the Wall at the End of the World could be entrusted to the gem giants. The zoogs could obtain meat without fretting over negotiations, too. This method would keep the gem giants in a steady supply of glass and help them avoid starvation.

"Should the gem giants ever discover a new vein of jewels, the stones can be added to the deal. If the zoogs' business comprehension grows, they should become comfortable enough to trade their liquor and mushrooms. With a profitable trade route for merchants along Zoltan's eastern road, the Merchants Guild will invest some money in dealing with the goblins and other monsters, making things safer for the villages along the way."

Mistorm nodded. "Hmm, if I ask a trader I know who could get some work for Godwin, too…I think this just might work."

"That would be great! It would take care of everything!" Mogrim clapped. He was as happy as if it had been his own problem solved. The dwarf gleefully detailed the plan to the gem giants, who grasped the concept and stomped the ground in joy.

The chief proclaimed, "Little friend, blessings' guide, may your journey be always graced with light!"

That feast was when I learned that gem giants had a habit of singing to express their joy.

Chapter 6

- - - - - - - - -

Journey's End and the Beginning of the Solstice Festival

""We're back,"" we said as we opened the door.

Of course, there was no one waiting in our shop.

Rit and I looked at each other and grinned.

""Welcome back!""

"Phew, shall we take care of the bags?"

"Sounds good."

We set our bags down and unpacked the dirty clothes, leftover rations, and whatever else.

"I never did get a blue sapphire...," I muttered.

Mogrim had said everything had worked out, yet there was still no stone for Rit's engagement ring.

"But it was fun," Rit replied as she hugged me. "We had lunch together out in the meadows, entered monster villages, saw beautiful scenery, met old friends! And even got to visit a hot spring together! There were lots of smiles!"

"You're right. I had fun." I hugged Rit back and then hesitated, unsure whether to say what I was thinking or not.

"What is it?" Rit asked. She always knew when I was troubled.

"The thing is, I had intended to use the blue agate I'd placed on hold if I couldn't get a blue sapphire for your ring, but..."

Blue sapphire suited Rit far better.

"At first, I thought it would be okay. However, after seeing Mogrim refuse to compromise for Mink and go all the way out to the Wall at the End of the World and come back with an iridescent ruby…"

"Yeah," Rit said with a nod.

"I started thinking that a quiet life isn't the sort of thing to be making compromises about. Even if we take the longer route and go at our own pace, the point is to spend our days the way we desire. That's why…I was hoping you could wait just a little longer on the ring. I don't want to make concessions when it comes to something for you."

"I understand," Rit responded immediately.

"Is that really okay?"

"Of course it is! You're putting so much thought into it, after all."

"How could I not? This is for my Rit."

"Eh-heh-heh. Then it's fine. I'll wait. And besides." Rit paused to look into my eyes. "While I'm waiting, we'll still be together, right?"

"Always."

The two of us remained embracing each other for a short while until Rit suddenly looked up. "Shall we take a bath together? It's just the two of us now, so it's fine, right?"

"Y-yeah, let's," I responded.

Even though we'd just returned from a journey together, seeing Rit's happy smile felt more like coming home than walking through the door to the pharmacy had.

The winter sky was clear and blue as far as the eye could see.

Today was the winter solstice festival for the continent of Avalon.

It was a celebration held during the shortest day of the year. It was a holiday where the new winter demon was cast away and pork, bread, and wine were offered up to Demis and Victy along with prayers for peace and a bountiful harvest.

"Are you ready, Rit?"

"Yep, I'm coming out now."

She poked her head out from the bedroom after changing.

"How do I look?"

Blushing, she performed a little spin to show off the dress she was wearing. The hem of the skirt flared up a bit, revealing a glimpse of thigh.

"It looks great on you," I declared.

"Eh-heh-heh." Rit hugged me happily.

Today, she was wearing a silk scarf around her neck instead of her usual bandana. The ends dangling down her chest were embroidered with vibrant flowers that worked really well with her whole ensemble.

"Your coat suits you well, Red."

"Really?"

Seeing me redden slightly, Rit beamed, slipped her arms around my waist, and pressed her breasts against my side. My heart started pounding from that soft sensation, and, when she realized that, Rit's smile widened.

"It was nearly the winter solstice when you left Loggervia, wasn't it?" I recalled.

Rit nodded. "Now that you mention it, yeah."

"I restrained myself then, but I really wanted to spend the festival with you in Loggervia."

At the time, we'd had to move on to the next battle after having saved Loggervia. Our journey took us to Seren, the gateway to Cataphract Kingdom. We had heard rumors about agitators pushing to reject all cooperation with Avalonia there and needed to resolve that. It had been a bloody solstice fighting with insurgents spurred on by demons, and I preferred not to remember it.

"All right, shall we go enjoy the celebration?" I suggested.

"Yeah!"

Rit released her grip on my waist and immediately slipped her arms around my left one. "Mm… Okay, let's go!"

I hesitated for a moment, but we'd look fine during the festivities as we were.

*   *   *

It was said that if you failed to drive out the winter demon, the cold would last longer, and the spring harvest would be bad. Those tasked with repelling the winter demon were a Drake Rider and Saint with Victy's blessing.

In this case, the Drake Rider was a person on a float adorned with glittering scales and made to look like a gold drake. The Saint bore a trident—Victy's holy symbol—and chased off the winter demon, represented by someone wearing a goat mask. The roles were played by villagers, this being a tradition that had lasted for many years.

Many people played the Drake Rider and Saint throughout the day, but the person playing the winter demon remained the same. They wore a heavy costume and spent all day walking around, dancing wildly, and running amok. So by the end of the day, they would be exhausted and hardly able to move. At that point, the Drake Rider would stab the winter demon with its sword, and the demon would stumble out of the town.

Basically, everyone had to spend the whole day dancing, singing, and playing to wear the demon out.

"Hey, Red! Having fun?" Gonz called. He was already red faced and a bit drunk. Tanta was beside him, excitedly struggling to deal with a big piece of sugared bread.

"Hey, Gonz, looks like you're in a good mood," I replied.

"Of course! It's a festival. Everyone's off work. And I'm taking tomorrow off for the hangover!"

"Tomorrow, too?"

"Who can work in this cold?"

Some people said that half-elves were all diligent, but that was not the case for those in Zoltan.

Tanta looked inspired by Gonz's hearty proclamation. "You tell them, Uncle!"

Uh-oh—at this rate, Tanta's going to grow up to be a good-for-nothing adult.

"I'm going to be back on the job tomorrow, Tanta," I said.

"Ehhh? C'mon, just take the day off. I wanna go fishing with everyone," Gonz whined.

Rit's face lit up at that. "Oooh, that sounds fun."

"Right?!" Gonz answered.

"Uh, Rit…," I called, to no avail.

Gonz's suggestion had caught her interest, and the two of them and Tanta started chanting, "Take a break!"

Cut it out, you guys; people will stare!

Finally, I caved. "I got it. I got it. All of Zoltan will be lying around tomorrow anyway, so we can go fishing at the river."

""""Yay!""""

Gonz and Rit were frolicking around with their hands in the air like Tanta.

Sheesh…

"Yay."

Just then, I heard a calm voice from behind me, mimicking the cheers. Turning around, I saw Ruti and Tisse with their hands up—their faces blank as usual.

"Eh, you two are taking tomorrow off, too?" I questioned.

"Of course. If Big Brother is, then so am I."

"It would be unfair if we were the only ones working."

Oh no. Ruti and Tisse have become good-for-nothings.

"Tomorrow's shaping up to be fun," Rit remarked.

I relaxed my shoulders and smiled.

Well, fine, I guess. This is Zoltan, after all. Getting lazy once in a while isn't so bad.

"Yeah, it should be."

Seeing me nod, the layabouts all cheered again.

*　　　　　*　　　　　*

Different parts of Zoltan had distinct cultures, so checking out how the celebration changed from neighborhood to neighborhood was part of the fun.

The streets of the working-class section were lined with stalls. You could find meat skewers, fish, fries, bacon-and-lettuce sandwiches, sugary sweets, sweet breads, carved wooden toys, and even second-hand odds and ends for sale, though not for particularly low prices.

"See you later. We're gonna look for Nao and Mido," said Gonz.

Tanta waved to us. "See ya, Big Bro. You can be as lovey-dovey as you want today, and I won't laugh!"

"How rude. When have I ever been like that?" I shot back.

"When are you ever not?"

Tanta and Gonz laughed and headed toward a plaza where the sound of a lute could be heard.

"Ha. All right, want to get something to eat?" I asked.

"Yeah," Rit answered with a nod.

Ruti briskly walked up to my right side and grabbed my hand. "I want to hold hands, too," she stated, blushing ever so slightly.

"Sure. Shall we go, then?"

To my left, Rit and I had our arms entwined, and to my right, Ruti was holding my hand. I couldn't help but feel slightly embarrassed as we drew gazes from all sides.

*　　　　　*　　　　　*

"We were supposed to meet up here, but…"

Rit, Ruti, Tisse, and I were looking around the bustling plaza.

"Ah, there!" a lively voice shouted over the crowd as a bob of golden hair peeked out from the throng. Yarandrala wove her way through the crowd toward us.

"Phew, I'm glad you found us," I greeted her.

Yarandrala breathed a little sigh of relief. Unlike us, she was wearing her usual clothes. Perhaps noticing my gaze, she puffed her cheeks out a bit.

"I really wanted to wear a dress, but there wasn't any time at all."

"Yeah, trying to get something made on such short notice would be impossible. But your earrings look lovely on you," I complimented her.

Yarandrala's face brightened at that.

"Sharp as ever, Red. I'm glad you noticed."

The high elf had still tried to fit the mood despite not having an outfit ready by changing her accessories. Earrings with gems embedded in them were dangling from her long ears.

"There really are a lot of humans here. I didn't know it would be this lively, given how far out in the countryside Zoltan is."

"Ah-ha-ha, even out in the sticks, celebrations are fun. And it's not just humans, either." I pointed to a float being pulled by local dwarves on which a dwarf was acting out a fight with a drake. "Dwarves, half-elves, high elves, and all the other demi-humans living in Zoltan are all enjoying the festival, too."

Mogrim was sitting atop the float.

"And then the heroic dwarf thrust his ax into the single weak point in the demonic drake's scaly hide!" He rang a bell while recounting dwarven tales. "And then!"

He turned the handle on the side of the float. The drake split into two halves that fell to the side as a human woman wearing a dress emerged. The dwarven hero dropped the ax he was holding, and a bouquet of flowers appeared in his hand.

"As a reward, the dwarf who had become a hero received permission from his king to live with the woman he loved!" Mogrim proclaimed.

Applause rang out.

A float that could change scenes. That was dwarves for you. It really was an ingenious display.

"I didn't know dwarves were such big fans of romance," Yarandrala remarked.

"High elves and dwarves don't get many chances to share each other's cultures, do they?" I inquired.

"They do not. I've lived a long life, but there are still so many things I've yet to learn."

Pointing to a booth nearby, I said, "Would you care to know how the frankfurters from that food stall over there taste next?"

Yarandrala nodded emphatically. "Yes, please! Are they good?"

"Yep, they're exquisite!"

"Then let's go now before people start to line up!" Yarandrala excitedly grabbed my hand.

*   *   *

In the harbor district, the crews of the various moored ships celebrated in their own cultures' ways, all having a raucous good time.

"Oh, that's a Veronian party. He's probably from the Kubashin tribal lands."

A brown-skinned sailor was twirling a harpoon while dancing on a little stage. It was a dance performed by the people of southern Kubashin.

"You know about Kubashin, Big Brother? We never went there when we were traveling together, though," Ruti said.

"When I was with the knights, I had a mission to dispatch a dust dragon out there. We were sent to deal with it and support the pro-Avalonia faction in Kubashin."

When the Kingdom of Veronia was expanding its influence and territory under its pirate king, many neighboring smaller countries had hoped to establish friendly relations with the Flamberge Kingdom and the Kingdom of Avalonia to protect against Veronian aggression.

Prior to the demon lord's invasion, the nobles and assemblies of many countries had believed that the Kingdom of Veronia was a menace to the continent of Avalon.

"Kubashin is a state split by the sea. It's both an island and a port on the continent. The two combined into a single state due to their close economic and cultural relations. There are at least ten ferries back and forth between the island and the mainland every day, carrying people and goods," I explained.

The harpoon the sailor was holding was the symbolic weapon of his home. The region had developed around fishing, and unlike those in other lands, the bold Kubashin fishermen even hunted sea drakes.

It was a practice that had led to many deaths, but there had been a time when only those who had rowed themselves out alone on the seas and slain a sea drake solo were considered worthy of becoming the leader of Kubashin. The harpoon was the armament used for those ventures.

Nowadays, authority was granted by vote, but as part of the ceremony for taking the role, the new leader would fish along the coastal waters as the captain of a rowing ship to honor the old ways.

"Huh. I only knew the name as a place on a map, but it has quite the history," Ruti commented.

Nodding, I answered, "Every town does."

Naturally, that went for Zoltan, too.

"Ruti! Tisse!" someone called.

A high elf leaped out of the *oden* stall.

"Oparara."

It was the high elf who ran the *oden* shop. Ruti and Tisse had helped her out a while back, and they'd remained friends.

Oparara wrapped each of the other two girls in a warm embrace. And then she noticed Yarandrala.

"Oh, a high elf I've never met before…"

"I'm Yarandrala. It's nice to meet you, Oparara."

"G-good evening, Ms. Yarandrala. It is an honor to meet an elf of the hallowed city."

Something was a bit off.

"What's up with you, Oparara?" I questioned.

Oparara grabbed my shoulder forcefully and pulled me away from Yarandrala before switching to a quiet whisper.

"You never told me you knew a Kiramin elf, boss!"

"A Kiramin elf?"

"We high elves refer to each other by where we're from. I was born in Zoltan, so I'm a Zoltan elf, and Ms. Yarandrala there is from Kiramin, so she's a Kiramin elf!"

"I'm amazed you can tell where she was born."

"Us high elves just sort of recognize it in each other! Anyway, Kiramin elves are special! She's not going to think I'm just some country bumpkin for being born in the sticks, is she?"

"I think it will be fine. Yarandrala's a good friend of mine, and she's been living outside of Kiramin longer than within it."

"Hey!" Yarandrala called out to us. "Oparara, I was born in Kiramin, but that doesn't mean anything."

"Y-yes, ma'am."

"Besides, I like Zoltan. Even though I came here to invite Red and the others to come with me to Kiramin, they liked Zoltan enough to say they'd rather stay here."

"Yes, ma'am! This is indeed a great place! I don't know anywhere else, and I'm sure it can't begin to compare to Kiramin's beauty and bravery, but I love this town!" Suddenly realizing what she'd said, Oparara blushed and looked down.

If I remembered correctly, Oparara was about forty-five. She conducted herself fairly maturely, but that evidently wasn't the case around Yarandrala.

It was Oparara's first time meeting a high elf from a different town, so it was interesting to see her reaction.

"Yarandrala," Ruti cut in, seeing Oparara looking troubled. "Oparara is an amazing elf who makes really delicious *oden*. You should try it."

"Really? I'd love to!"

"I can't say whether it would befit the palate of an elf from the hallowed city, though..."

"It's okay, Oparara. Yarandrala is my friend. There's no need for friends to speak like that with each other."

"But—"

"Ruti's right. I'd like to enjoy it to the fullest."

"Y-yes, ma'am! I'd be honored!"

"That's not how you normally speak while running your shop, is it? Don't mind me, prepare your food as you usually would. If you don't, how will I ever learn what *oden* in Zoltan is really like?"

When she heard that, Oparara's expression tensed. She had taken over this cart from its old master because she loved it and didn't want to see it disappear once the master retired. Her dedication was by no means trifling.

"Understood… If you're going to say that much, it'd be rude not to! The stand's right this way! Grab yourselves a seat!"

Oparara still appeared a little nervous, but she had at least managed to get back to her normal style.

Yarandrala grinned, evidently enjoying herself as we grabbed seats at the stall.

"So you're parked here today?" I inquired.

"Festival decorations occupy the place where I usually set up," Oparara replied.

"Huh."

"So what'll you have? I've got some nice octopus today. And the fish balls are particularly great, too."

Octopus oden?

"Interesting. I'll try that. And some burdock, too," I said.

My sister spoke up next. "I'll have the octopus and some egg."

Then came Tisse. "I'll have the same as Ms. Ruti as well as fish balls, squid balls, daikon, and two *chikuwa*, please."

Rit struggled to decide before settling on octopus, burdock, egg, fish balls, squid balls, daikon, and beef tendon.

"That's a pretty big order," I commented.

Rit pouted slightly. "They all seemed so good."

"What about you, Yarandrala?" I asked.

"I'll have what Red is having. Octopus and burdock, and some fish balls as well, please."

"Gotcha!" Oparara acknowledged.

We requested some alcohol as well. Rit was a little tipsy as she eagerly chowed down. Tisse enthusiastically enjoyed her *chikuwa* in her own way. She looked satisfied.

"Delicious," Ruti remarked.

"It really is! This is a flavor you can't find in Kiramin," Yarandrala chimed in.

Oparara flashed a gratified smile at their compliments.

The plan had been to just have a quick visit, but before I realized it, we had ordered seconds.

"That reminds me, you've gotten more seafood on the menu lately," I remarked.

"Yeah, more of it has been passing through the port recently, so I've been able to get good-quality ingredients at a better price, which has been a big help," Oparara responded.

"Huh."

"Winter fish tastes fantastic. It's not *oden*, but I can grill you some if you like."

"That sounds great."

It was a full lunch course.

Hanging out at an *oden* stall, relaxing and enjoying drink and food—talk about a luxurious slow life!

Oparara pulled out a few of the coals warming the *oden*, slipped them into a stove, and set a metal mesh on top. Then she skillfully prepared a fatty *isaki* fish, dried it with a cloth, and sprinkled it with salt. Zoltan salt wasn't famous or anything, but it was pretty high quality if you asked me.

Then she placed a salted slice of fish on top of the mesh. There was a whoosh of steam as the scent of a delicious fillet of fish being grilled filled the air.

"Order up."

The meat on the plate was grilled to a scrumptious brown.

"It looks great," Ruti said, quickly breaking off a little with her fork to try.

"What do you think?" Oparara questioned.

Ruti's eyes wavered in silence.

"Really? Great! I'll whip up another for you, on the house!"

Oparara understood just from that.

She was already hard at work cooking more.

"That's nice," Rit commented, watching Ruti and the others with a kind smile.

"Yeah, it sure is," I agreed.

*   *   *

We hung around the harbor district for longer than we'd intended, but there was still plenty of time.

"Oh yeah, where's the winter demon?" Rit asked.

Putting a hand to my chin, I responded, "Around now, it's supposed to be in the northside, I think?"

The festival's leading role, that of the winter demon, followed a set schedule and route. Though with Zoltan's usual pace, it was only ever an estimate.

"We had a nice lunch, so let's head downtown since that's next after northside, and we can just relax and take it easy there," I suggested.

Rit nodded. "Yeah, that sounds good."

"Great, it's settled."

Normally, everyone would be bundled up and hiding away at home to avoid the cold, but today the whole town was out celebrating in the streets.

One of the guards was putting on a great performance with a trumpet, and some thieves from Southmarsh were dancing lightheartedly to the music. Members of the Mages Guild were shooting off dragon fireworks that dashed through the sky, while a bunch of children who typically hated studying were pestering them for a lecture on how they did it.

A group of half-orcs drummed to a beat as they walked around. Coupled with a three-stringed instrument, it made for quite a cheerful sound. Behind were a bunch of young humans, who commonly looked down on half-orcs. They were having fun dancing along.

Rounding the corner, I spotted half-elves playing bright, refreshing music on their wooden flutes. Even the downtown aristocrats stopped in their tracks to listen. A bowl out in front of them was flipped over to show they didn't need any tips today. The crowd encircling the half-elves offered thunderous applause instead.

"Thank you," one said before returning to his flute.

✳   ✳   ✳

"Hm? Isn't that Godwin?"

"Oh, yeah. Is he really okay to be just walking around like that without hiding his face or anything? And his clothes are kind of elegant compared to before."

Yarandrala and I had noticed Godwin milling among the throngs of revelers with a beer in his hand.

"Hmm? Oh! If it isn't Red, Rit, Ruti, Tisse, and Yarandrala..."

Noticing us, Godwin staggered a little unsteadily over our way. Mister Crawly Wawly, who was riding on Tisse's shoulder, raised one of his front legs when Godwin made it to us.

Godwin raised his glass in response. "Hey there, Mister Crawly Wawly." The man's consummate bad guy's face cracked into a broad smile. "Ha-ha, make sure you enjoy Zoltan's festival, too, buddy."

"Hey, I know Mistorm is doing something to sweep your crimes under the table, but should you really be wandering around town this openly?" I questioned.

"Heh-heh-heh. The lame old crook you knew is gone," Godwin responded, flashily pointing to the area below the collar of his shirt.

My eyes went wide at the sight of what was there. "Isn't that a Merchants Guild badge? You're a merchant now?"

I was also a member of that organization. I didn't make a point of wearing it usually, but I had the pin in storage back home.

"Yep! I don't gotta do any sneaking around in the shadows to make my money now! I'm gonna run the trade between Zoltan and the zoogs." Godwin puffed his chest out proudly.

"Ohhhh. Yeah, if it's you, there shouldn't be any problems with the monsters near the roads out that way, and the zoogs know your face," I said.

"And as a former affiliate of the Thieves Guild and associate of Bighawk's faction, I can stare down any guys who might try to horn in on my business."

Godwin probably didn't have the insight to find new sales opportunities, but in that sense, maybe he was the ideal fit for the job.

"From here on out, no more shadows for me. I'm gonna walk out in the open sun as a respectable broker."

The man seemed to be enjoying himself, but when Yarandrala stepped closer, his smile froze.

"Wh-what is it...?"

"Godwin."

"Y-yes, ma'am...?"

Yarandrala clenched her fist. Immediately, a look of terror spread across Godwin's face. A ring of yellow flowers appeared in Yarandrala's hand.

"Congratulations. I'll be praying for your success."

"Ah, huh?" Godwin was dumbstruck as he accepted the blossoms. "Y-yeah. Thanks."

Never had he expected the high elf to offer her support. Nervously, Godwin scratched his head.

"Heh-heh-heh. A little encouragement ain't half-bad," he said with a grin.

*   *   *

There were five churches in Zoltan, one in each district.

Excluding the one downtown, they were just simple wooden structures, like normal houses modified slightly. That's not to suggest they were inappropriate, however. Neither Demis nor the three disciples demanded extravagance from their places of worship. Even Southmarsh's chapel, dilapidated as the homes around it, was fine in the eyes of God.

"But then why do people want to build such opulent shrines?"

We were waiting outside the church downtown for the winter demon. There was a big group of people there, all hoping to join the dance with the winter demon.

Zoltan's central place of worship was large, with two steeples, and the main hall had an arched ceiling. The expensive stained glass gave it a majestic air, and paintings and sculptures with religious motifs lined the walls.

"Something this big wasn't made by a Zoltan architect," I commented.

"For sure," Rit agreed.

Construction had required Zoltan authorities to hire a foreign architect.

Taking in the sight, I said, "It's still on the simple side compared to the cathedral in the capital, though."

Tisse's spider hopped from his spot on the girl's shoulder.

"Mister Crawly Wawly says that it looks like a building that would be fun to climb."

"Ha-ha-ha. It must seem like an obstacle course to him," I answered.

We laughed a bit as Mister Crawly Wawly tilted his head and did a playful dance.

"It's probably...," Ruti began as she looked up at the church. "It's probably because *we* need it. Not because God does."

I turned to face my sister. "The extravagant church?"

"We can't perceive beautiful things in places that aren't beautiful. God doesn't mind any location, but we need an acceptable place to pray. That's what I think."

I looked up at the engraving set above the entrance to the church. It depicted seven devils cowering in fear of Demis's light and fleeing.

"The seven devils who rejected Demis's Divine Blessing," I muttered.

The story went that they had tried to get humanity to deny their Divine Blessings and thus throw the world into chaos. For this action, the demons were cast into the seven circles of hell, where they suffered eternal punishment. It was believed that some of the demons had possessed female forms. This quickly became an excuse for artists to depict the nude female body in public spaces.

While we were looking at the church, I heard someone opening the door and walking with a staff.

"Oh, so you're here, too," remarked an aged voice.

Facing the sound, I said, "Mistorm."

She was wearing the same plain, unadorned silver silk robe she'd had on the trip despite being surrounded by nobles sporting the latest styles from Central.

"Ruti, Tisse, and Yarandrala, this is your first time experiencing Zoltan's winter festival, right? Make sure to enjoy yourselves," she urged.

"I already am. Zoltan is an interesting town. There were lovely performances by humans, elves, dwarves, even orcs. It's been a wonderful collection of firsts," answered Tisse.

Yarandrala bobbed her head in agreement. "Our races might be different, but the one thing we all have in common is that everyone present is a stray who ended up here after starting somewhere else."

Apparently, those two had fought during their first meeting, but that was hard to imagine when one saw them casually chat.

"Whoopsie, I've got more company. I'm going to be barhopping with all sorts of folk," Mistorm stated with a shrug and a grin.

"I don't think anyone other than you would call visits with nobles barhopping," I quipped.

"What else would you call going out to drink with old friends in familiar places?"

I frowned for a moment and then conceded the point. "I guess so."

"Ha-ha-ha, I'm just a retired old lady who hardly ever makes an appearance, so I appreciate them not forgetting me and inviting me along. And delicious free booze is always nice. Anyway, it would be rude for me to keep them waiting much longer, so pardon me."

"Okay, don't partake too much," I cautioned.

"I'm a veteran when it comes to that! …The trip was fun. We should have a drink or two and share some stories from the road sometime."

Mistorm waved before heading back to the nobles.

She was Zoltan's former mayor, the previous head of the Zoltan Mages Guild, and the leader of last generation's B-rank adventurers. It had been a pleasure to travel with that Zoltan hero.

"Yes, it was a lovely journey," Yarandrala muttered, as though to echo my thoughts.

"Ah! Red! The winter demon's here!" Rit shouted from behind us.

"Oh."

The winter demon with its goat head and body covered in black cloth had come. It wasn't really staggering, either. For someone who had been dancing since morning, those were some solid, mighty footsteps. The winter demon this year had respectable endurance.

The float holding the Drake Rider and the Saint was chasing after it.

"Wait, wait! Hail, winter demon! Face me in combat!"

The Drake Rider gestured defiantly before leaping down from the papier-mâché drake head and spun his prop spear. It was a pretty dangerous move, but the winter demon made a show of evading it playfully, leaping around and dodging.

"Moving around that well while dressed up like that's pretty impressive," I observed.

While the Drake Rider was only wearing papier-mâché armor painted a woody brown, the winter demon costume had a mask made from a goat's skull, and the body was crafted of thick cloth, either of which should have limited the wearer's mobility. Yet the winter demon's movements were enchantingly rhythmic and fluid. The Drake Rider was energetic and vigorous, but you couldn't help but feel like he was being toyed with, and before long, people were starting to laugh.

Just then, the Drake Rider glanced toward our group and froze. "Hm?"

Wait, that voice sounds familiar.

"Ohh! It's my beloved Valkyrie!"

The Drake Rider dashed over to Ruti with a thudding gait. He removed his helmet, revealing a bearded face.

Ruti met his eager gaze evenly. "…Who are you?"

"I-it is I! The knight whom you traded blows with on the bridge!"

"???"

Oh, I remember now. He was that nuisance warrior who had been blocking the bridge. Otto, I think?

However, Ruti didn't seem to recall him at all. She furrowed her brow.

"Ms. Ruti, he's the one you threw under the bridge when we were on our way to Zoltan," said Tisse.

"Ah." Ruti plopped her fist on her palm.

"Oh, so you've finally remembered me! I am the Otto the Drake Rider. Commander of the glorious Fafnir Knights' first company."

"No, I just vaguely recalled something like that happening. I don't remember your face or anything about you at all."

That's a bit harsh, Ruti. He's going to get depressed.

Undaunted, Otto continued, "Still, for us to meet again here is truly fate. The guidance of Almighty Demis. Now, let us join hands and defeat the winter demon. Then we shall slay the hill giant Dundach and become nobles together!" Otto held out his hand.

I was the one who grabbed his arm, however.

"Hey there."

"What are...?! You're that coward!"

"Tell me again, who was the coward?"

"What could be more dastardly than attacking an opponent unawares!"

"No, you definitely struck first. You were naked, as I recall."

The mere thought of that day was exasperating. Also, while I had grabbed Otto's arm because I didn't want him touching Ruti, it was also for his own safety.

"...Grr..."

Ruti was clearly displeased, though Otto surely couldn't tell. If he had tried to touch her, he would have gotten knocked away pretty mightily. It would have just been a push, but a shove from the strongest person in the world was nothing to dismiss. Even in the best case, Otto would have gone flying into the wall across the plaza, broken every bone in his body, and had to undergo a months-long recovery course.

"Release me, coward, if you know what is best for you," the Drake Rider insisted.

"Hmph."

"Owww!!!"

Otto tried to break away, but I exerted pressure on his elbow. Tears started to well up in his eyes as he desperately tapped my arm in surrender.

"I—I give! I give!"

"It's not like this is a contest."

"Wh-what are you even mad about?"

"I'm not mad."

"Eeeep!"

The crowd around us started laughing as Otto cried out pathetically.

Not good, we're standing out too much.

Unwilling to make more of a scene, I released him.

"D-dastard! Face me in a fair fight!"

"Very well."

What did I do to deserve this?

Rit and Ruti started doing warm-up stretches—Yarandrala, too.

It's overkill already. If the three of you join in, there won't be anything left of him.

Just then, an enormous shadow appeared behind Otto. It was the winter demon.

"Hgh?!"

Its big hand hit Otto on the top of the head with a thud.

That single blow was enough to send the man crashing to the ground. Then the winter demon grabbed Otto by the scruff of the neck and dragged him away.

"Wait, is that Danan?" I wondered aloud.

Hearing that, the winter demon turned around and winked through the mask.

He's supposed to be recovering! What's he doing?!

Back in the center of the plaza, the Saint started hitting Otto over and over, evidently upset at him for going off on his own. The comical act drew a big laugh and cheers from the crowd.

*   *   *

In the evening, the exhausted winter demon—though he didn't look fatigued at all—fled the town, and the festival finally reached its finale.

Everyone was supposed to revel in these final hours as much as possible in hopes of spring arriving even one day sooner.

Nothing better suited Zoltan's mentality than putting one's all into living in the moment, even during the dead of winter. It really felt like the celebration was the seasonal event that everyone here got the most excited for.

"Hey, look. The baron's kid is dancing over there."

"No way! Maybe I should go, too!"

"Let's all go! Maybe we can marry into money!"

Three young women scurried after the bachelor. It sounded like one of them was planning for the future.

While I watched, Yarandrala tapped my shoulder.

"Red, Rit, Ruti, Tisse, Mister Crawly Wawly. Thank you for today. It was great fun."

"Hmm, going back to the inn already?" I asked.

The high elf shook her head. "No, I was thinking of checking in on a friend first."

"A friend? Ahh, okay. It was fun to enjoy a festival with you again after so long."

"I had fun chatting with you, Yarandrala. But there are still many more things about Red I want to discuss, so let's have lunch together sometime, just the two of us!" Rit said.

"I couldn't do this sort of thing when I was the Hero. I'm glad I got to know things about you that I didn't before," Ruti stated.

"Mister Crawly Wawly says he enjoyed our time together. And I did as well," Tisse added.

Yarandrala beamed. "Yes. I'll be staying in Zoltan for a little while, so let's do something again soon."

As Yarandrala took her leave, she kept turning back to wave reluctantly.

✳   ✳   ✳

The sun hung low on the horizon, threatening to sink beyond it at any moment.

The people of Zoltan were still dancing, reluctant to let the light end today's revelry.

Mister Crawly Wawly was riding on the back of Tisse's hand, and she was watching him as he danced around between her fingers. They stuck to their own pace, but they were having fun, judging from their expressions.

As I watched Tisse, I felt a tug at my clothes.

"Thank you for today, Big Brother," Ruti said with a smile. "It was fun."

I patted her head.

"There's still one thing left that we haven't done, though," I told her. "Eh?"

I took Ruti's hand. She reddened slightly.

"May I have this dance?"

"With you? ...Can I...?"

"There's nothing wrong with siblings sharing a dance."

Ruti looked over to Rit, who grinned and waved for her to go ahead.

"But the last time I danced at a winter festival was before you joined the knights. I don't know the steps very well."

I tugged Ruti's hand gently.

"The point isn't to move well. It's to enjoy yourself."

Demons supposedly hated joy. Of course, having fought the demon lord's army ourselves, we knew that was just a superstition. Even so, it gave us a reason to relish the moment, so there wasn't any need to debate that point.

"Shall we?"

"...Yes."

Ruti appeared a little unsure for a moment, but she accepted my offer.

The Zoltan musicians were striking up a jaunty spring song. The half-elves were playing flutes of a style rumored to have been created by wood elves. The instrument's proper name had not survived, though, and it was commonly referred to as an elven flute.

Wood elf culture hadn't been concerned with record keeping, so little was known about them. However, according to documents written by humans, wood elves had composed and played flute music as a dedication to their lovers. That custom was not still practiced by half-elves, however. These days, the instruments were just the source of beautiful sounds and nothing more.

Ruti and I danced a simple, fun step in time with the rhythm of the music, hands clasped all the while. My little sister's face was crimson, but she seemed to be delighted.

"Is this okay?" she asked.

"Is what?"

"Can I really be forgiven for being this happy?"

"You've suffered so much for the sake of so many people. It's about time you got to experience some joy for yourself."

Ruti's eyes remained trained on me as we strutted. I slipped my hands around her waist, lifting and spinning her.

I had always wanted Ruti to find her bliss. She had been my sister long before ever being the Hero. Seeing her wounded during fights had been terrible, serving as a constant reminder of my powerlessness to aid her.

"Big Brother...tha—"

"Thank you, Ruti," I cut in before she could offer her gratitude.

"Huh?"

"Thank you for finding happiness."

"Ah...uh..."

Tears welled up in Ruti's eyes.

Epilogue

"How About We Sleep In Tomorrow?"

After parting ways with Yarandrala and then Ruti and Tisse, Rit and I returned home.

"The festival's finally over," Rit stated a little bit forlornly.

"There will be another one next year," I reminded her.

"Will we still be together by then?"

"We will."

"And the year after?"

"Definitely."

"Eh-heh-heh." Rit smiled happily and then slipped her arms around my neck. Then she closed her eyes and lifted her chin a bit. "Nh," she urged me on.

My heart raced a little at her adorable gesture as I leaned in and kissed her. When our lips parted, I saw her elated smile. Enduring the sudden impulse to keep kissing her, I reached into my pocket and pulled out a little box.

"What's that?" Rit asked.

"A present."

"For me? Can I open it now?"

I took a half step back to give her space to take the box.

"A necklace! And this is a diamond, right?!"

It was indeed. The chain was pink gold, gold alloyed with silver and copper. As the name implied, it had a rosy gleam due to the copper.

"I got Mogrim to make the chain," I said.

"But what about the diamond?" Rit questioned.

"The truth is, during the fight with the gem beast, one of its gems got caught in my pocket. All of the other jewels turned to lead, but when the gem beast collapsed, Yarandrala and I were falling down the cliff, remember? Because of that, this one was spared."

Rit took the piece of jewelry in her hand.

"Well, umm, I promised to give you an engagement ring someday. For now, this is the best I can manage. Think of it as a down payment to show my determination to get a ring before too long."

"So it's an engagement necklace?"

"Basically."

Rit placed the thing in my hand, and I wondered if she didn't like it.

"Put it on for me."

"Ah, ahhh. Okay. I got it."

I slipped the necklace around Rit's neck and fastened the clasp. I could feel her breath on my neck, filling my heart with love and a ticklish embarrassment.

"How is it?" she asked.

I nodded. "It suits you well… It looks lovely."

"Ahh!" Rit leaped at me, burying her face in my chest. "You're so unfair!"

"Unfair…?"

"Saying that you'll get a ring for me later while giving a present like this! It isn't fair! I love you!" Rit clung to me. "You better take responsibility for making me feel this way."

"How should I do that?"

Rit moved her lips next to my ear. "…How about we sleep in tomorrow?"

A mesmerizing thrill of pleasure raced through me.

"You're no fair, either."

Somewhere along the way, I had started hugging Rit back. Awash in the warmth of her body, I was truly grateful we were able to share this kind of happy existence.

$$* \qquad * \qquad *$$

Darkness and silence fell upon Zoltan's harbor district. The festival had ended.

Revelers had either gone home or found their way to taverns to enjoy after-parties.

"Ha, nobles are always so damn longwinded at meals." The Archmage Mistorm leaned slightly on her walking stick as she moved along the street. "Still, the food was good. It's hard to believe that little brat Will is governor-general now."

The young boy who was always causing his parents problems and had once told anyone who would listen he would go to the capital and join the Bahamut Knights was now the commander of Zoltan's army. That scrawny kid had grown into a dignified middle-aged man. The stilted manner of speaking he'd adopted when trying to copy the stereotypical knight had developed into a proper tenor. Yet when Mistorm shook his hand, she could feel how large it had grown from his constant sword practice—the vestige of a boy who'd dreamed of being a knight.

"It was a fun trip. I haven't really bothered to go out much lately since it is such a hassle, but making the effort was worthwhile." Mistorm placed her hand on her hip. "Agh…I've been keeping my lower body in shape, but a hike in the mountains does a number on the hips."

Fortunately, Mistorm had a proxy to handle trading with the gem giants and zoogs, so she would be able to get away with sitting in on a meeting or two.

"Godwin's always been a shrewd kiddo. He'll be a good fit for this kind of business."

Mistorm walked along toward the inn where she was staying, the night breeze rustling past.

She had chosen a place in the harbor district over downtown because more people would have recognized her there. Plus, strolling while watching the moon reflected on the river's surface went well with basking in old memories.

Mistorm continued down the empty road by herself for a little while.

Someone's following me.

The tail had first given themselves away a short while ago.

There was only a single, small residential house nearby. There were no lights on, so the residents were most likely out.

Mistorm discreetly formed a seal. Maintaining a spell just on the verge of activation was her specialty, and she relied on that technique more than any other.

He's realized that I've noticed! Such murderous intent! Is he out to kill me?!

The old woman had been retired for years now. That anyone would still be after her was a surprise. However, Mistorm was still a veteran adventurer who had honed her skills in countless battles.

When the assassin made their move, she conjured a brilliant flash of light. If the assailant was using a Night Vision skill, that would temporarily blind them.

The assassin remained undaunted and drew their sword without so much as flinching.

Their eyes are closed?! A Mind's Eye skill?! This one's pretty strong!

Mistorm completed the seal with her left hand, loosing the magic she had been maintaining.

"Thunder Blade!"

A giant, three-meter-long sword of white electricity appeared from her hand, running the assassin through. The man collapsed to the ground singed and smoking.

"I know that's not the only one!"

Mistorm whirled, swinging her Thunder Blade at two more assailants who had been closing in behind her. Her blade caught nothing but empty air, though.

They dodged from that close?!

The assassins had leaped into the air and were swinging their swords down at Mistorm from above.

"Release!"

In response to the old woman's cry, the Thunder Blade swelled and exploded. A storm of lightning bolts burst out from the sword, destroying the surroundings. The assailants, still midplunge, were caught defenseless.

Mistorm's strength lay in her various methods of controlling her magic power. With a single upper-tier spell, she could call upon her reserve magic for a strike or feint, as the situation demanded. Many of her fights had been won because of the unexpected effects she could produce.

"That's a legendary pirate for you, even if she has grown old. Took the others out, huh?"

As the explosion of lightning died down, the final assassin landed on the ground.

"Someone who knows my past, huh?" Mistorm muttered.

This was one of the assassins who had been diving at her. He should have been caught in the blast, too, but he showed no signs of injury.

An unpleasant sweat formed on Mistorm's forehead, but she did not have the leeway to wipe as she held her staff at the ready.

He doesn't look too concerned. I can't say that doesn't annoy me! I still haven't fully recovered my magic power yet. Upper-tier spells are off-limits, so what am I gonna do now?

This assailant was a soldier with a high blessing level—someone Mistorm had never seen in Zoltan. He was already in range to reach Mistorm with his sword, so even if she could cast greater spells, it wasn't a great spot to be. The assassin was grinning with the confidence of one who knew victory was assured.

"Thorn Bind!"

"What?!"

Briars entangled the man's body. Yarandrala stepped out of the darkness, glaring at the man.

"She is a friend of mine," Mistorm remarked.

As he struggled, the assailant said, "...No one said anything about someone like you being here..."

"Not sure what to tell you," Yarandrala replied with a shrug.

"Martial Art: Flame Escape!" A blaze engulfed the man's body, burning away the thorny vines. "Haaaaaah!!!"

Fire erupted at the man's shout, and when the smoke from the conflagration cleared, both he and the bodies of his defeated fellows were gone. Yarandrala considered giving chase but decided to prioritize Mistorm instead.

"Are you all right?" the high elf asked.

"Thanks to you, yes."

The two women scanned their surroundings, but the assassins were long gone.

"Who were they?" Yarandrala questioned.

Mistorm shook her head. "I was attacked out of the blue. Never got a good enough look to say."

"Any guesses?"

"I used to be Zoltan's mayor, but I've been retired for ages. What's the point in coming for my head now?" Mistorm shrugged.

Hearing that, Yarandrala's well-shaped eyebrows twitched. "I'm here because I was searching for you."

"For me?"

"Let me start by saying that I consider you a friend."

"I'm happy to hear that, but…"

"So long as it's within my power, I want to help you. I owe you for the problems I caused before."

"That's a pretty roundabout windup. So why exactly were you looking for me?" Mistorm pressed, her eyes locked with Yarandrala's.

The high elf did not turn away, meeting the gaze.

"Demon's Flare, the magic you used against that Meteo. That's dark magic employed by the demon lord's army. And not by just any members of their ranks, either. Only upper-tier demons are capable of it."

"…To think there was someone on this continent who knew of such things…," muttered Mistorm.

"With the war on, more and more people are becoming familiar with demonkind," Yarandrala cautioned.

"I'll have to watch myself," Mistorm responded with a wry smile.

Yarandrala's expression remained deadly serious as she continued. "Mistorm, you aren't just a hero out in the countryside. There's more to you than that."

"…"

"Just who are you?"

Mistorm put her hand on her chin and sank into thought, and Yarandrala made no effort to hurry her, waiting for the other woman to decide whether to trust her or not.

Unlike Red and the others, who had given up their quest to enjoy a slow life, Yarandrala was still a hero. Alone on the longest night of the year, she had chosen to act for her friends' beloved newfound home and for this unlikely companion shrouded in mysteries standing before her.

Afterword

To everyone who has picked up this book, thank you very much! I'm the author, Zappon.

We've reached the fifth volume of the series. With five books lined up together on a shelf, it's clear to see they occupy their own little spot.

In the fourth volume, the story reached a critical juncture. Ruti was freed from the Divine Blessing of the Hero. Book five begins with Yarandrala rejoining the cast. The story this time is entirely new, something that has never been published in the web version.

Red and friends have faced danger and adventure many times to save the world, but this is their first proper journey for themselves, and it was a more easygoing excursion. This story was about a quest where there was time to stop and enjoy the view.

Ruti fought together with her companions in the battles instead of employing her sacrificial, solo-play style from the fourth volume. That was a real joy for me to write.

Volume 5 also has a special edition that includes a drama CD. This afterword is the same for both versions, so there are probably people reading it who bought the special edition, too. I hope you enjoyed it!

Yuuichirou Umehara, Red's voice actor, gives such a smooth and cool delivery. Ayana Taketatsu, who voices Ruti, has this great ability to re-create Ruti's pacing and mood, and the way she idolizes Red is perfect. Saori Oonishi gives such a passionate performance as Chris, Red's former subordinate, too; I could go on about that forever. Let's not forget Yumiri Hanamori as Rit. She does a fantastic job throughout, but her words are especially priceless when Rit is slipping into bed while Red is sleeping!

Thank you to the voice actors who imbued the characters with such spirit and to all of the audio people who worked to assemble the drama CD. It is a wonderful production.

The manga version of this story by Ikeno Masahiro is being serialized in *Monthly Shounen Ace*. The second volume of the manga is currently on sale, and the way Rit's expressions shift from scene to scene is adorable. The happiness Red feels living with her really comes through. It's a wonderful manga that genuinely conveys how much they enjoy themselves in Zoltan.

Yarandrala made her reappearance in this volume of the light novel series, and she debuts in Volume 2 of the manga, as does her trump card.

If you enjoy these books, I highly recommend you give the manga a try! Next is Volume 6.

With the festival done, Zoltan will begin moving toward spring. Red and company will enjoy taking it easy in the second half of winter. I also intend to write more about Yarandrala and Mistorm, as well as Zoltan itself!

I hope you enjoy this world I've created and the happy lives that exist within it!

Once more, I'd like to point out that I wouldn't have gotten this far without the help of many people.

To Yasumo, your illustrations are always great. They were just as fantastic this time, too. Thank you for providing such lovely pictures for this book.

To the designers, proofreaders, printers, and everyone involved in the actual production, it is because of you that this work exists. Thank you very much.

To this series's editor, Miyakawa, it feels like we only started the other day, but our story has reached its fifth volume. I remember us worrying about how we would get readers interested, and yet here we are.

And finally, to all of you, if you got even a little bit of pleasure out of this book, then I've done my job. I hope you will continue to support this series in the future.

Zappon
Looking out on heavy spring rains, 2019

This is Yasumo. The illustrations were a joy to create! I keep practicing in the hope of improving so I can convey all the compelling scenes better.

An assassin's blade
trains on the mysterious
mage Mistorm!
What will Tisse do
in the face of these
rogue killers?!

Banished
FROM THE
Hero's
Party,
I Decided to Live a Quiet Life
in the Countryside

6